Dusty

ERIKSON BROTHERS BOOK 2

KATHI S. BARTON

This is a work of fiction. Names, characters, places, and incidents are products of the author's imagination or are used fictitiously and are not to be construed as real. Any resemblance to actual events, locations, organizations, or persons, living or dead, is entirely coincidental.

World Castle Publishing, LLC
Pensacola, Florida
Copyright © 2024 Kathi S. Barton
Paperback ISBN: 9798891262973
eBook ISBN: 9798891262980
First Edition World Castle Publishing, LLC, October 21, 2024
http://www.worldcastlepublishing.com
Licensing Notes
Cover: Cover Designs by Karen
Cover-designs-by-karen.com
Editor: Karen Fuller

Chapter 1

Shipley wasn't sure what to expect when she got off the big-bellied plane she'd been on. Telling her sister that she wasn't coming in commercial but on one of the planes that the army used had gotten her all mixed up. But she understood now. She'd been stressed for the last several months over things with her family. Not that it mattered too much how stressed she was. Shipley was going to make sure that no one took advantage of her baby sister—she was eighteen minutes younger than her.

Shipley was thrilled to be home. Even if it was for the funeral of her brother-in-law, Fred Landry. She had four weeks off, thanks to saving up her vacation time and all her paid time off. Her plan was to make every minute count, too.

While she hadn't particularly cared for Fred,

his mom was a nightmare. She knew that her sister was happy, and that was all she could have hoped for. Alma Landry was pushy and seemed to be pushing Fred into doing things that she was sure her sister would not approve of. Even during their wedding, the first time she'd been home to meet the family, Shipley decided that she was going to leave Amanda alone for the trouble that she might well have gotten into by stepping in where it was really none of her business.

"Candace?" She nearly didn't look in the direction that her name was called from. No one had called her by her first name in years. At least to anyone that she would answer to anyway. "There you are. I've missed you so much." The hugs were a welcome change from the salutes that she had been getting most of her adult life.

Mandy, Amanda's oldest little girl, was with her mom, and Shipley couldn't have been more happy. The kid was the spitting image of them when she and her sister had been little, and she had her no-bullshit kind of style about her. Shipley got hugs from them both and let out a long breath when she finally was with her sister.

"I've had to borrow a car. I didn't think you'd

have too much luggage—do you?" She told her that she only had her duffle, and it was in luggage claims. "You're armed too, I'm assuming?"

"Yes. Forever. You know that." She didn't point out that she was still a serviceman even though she was on a little break. "How about some lunch? My treat. I'm starving. And I want a meatball sub so bad that I'm nearly salivating for it."

She picked up her duffle, used to carrying it around when she moved. Shipley was a doctor for a M.A.S.H. unit, meaning mobile Army surgical hospital, unit that she'd been with since she'd gotten out of boot camp. Now, it was all she knew. Patching up men and women to get them either home or back on the front line. Usually not too far from where she was when working. But it was a good job and one that she dearly loved. Most of the time.

The place that they'd gone to eat when they were out of the large military airport wasn't too busy. Mandy, forever her buddy, said that she wanted to try a bite of her sub because she'd never had meatballs on anything but noodles. Grinning at her, she told the little girl that she'd have to fight her for it. Knowing full well that she'd give it all to her if she liked it.

After eating, stuffed too, the three of them sat in the booth and talked about all the things that had been going on since the last time she'd been home. Mostly, it was her talking, Amanda seemed to be wanting to vent, and she let her. It worried her that she was so freely speaking in front of Mandy but she'd bet the kid knew more than her mom was telling her about.

"Alma is out of our hair for now. I have a feeling, however, that she is going to bully someone into trying to hurt us some other way. I did tell you that she tried to kidnap the kids right out from under my nose, didn't I?" She looked so sad then that she reached out and took her hand into hers. "I had no idea the lengths that she'd go about to take the kids from me. To think that she…Alma actually came into my home and tried to take them without permission, Candace. Who does that sort of thing? That is going to get her in the most trouble. Attempted kidnapping is what I think that they're calling it. But she won't be out of jail for a long time, I'm hoping."

"If not, then I'll take care that you're safe."

She eyed her hard and Shipley didn't say a word. She was used to being second-guessed, as she assumed her sister was doing right now. "How about we get going? I could use a long shower and nap. I've been traveling since yesterday, and my underwear is sticking to all the wrong places."

"Gross, Aunt Candace." Mandy cocked her head and stared at her. "Does anyone call you Candy while you're at work? I'm betting that no one does."

"And you'd be correct. I've been known as Shipley for so long that I sometimes forget that I have a first name." She asked her why they called her that. "Because my dear niece, they don't call anyone by their first name because that would mean that you're close to them. And where I work, it's not something you want to do in the event that they're killed."

"Oh." She looked at her sister when she tsked at her. "It's all right, momma. I know that she is in the line of fire. I think that we're all lucky that she's able to come home to us. I saw that on a movie that I watched. They all were killed because some jerk called in an airstrike or something like that. It's sad, really."

"How old are you? Fifty? Sixty? You're the oldest kid I know, and that's saying a great deal. Christ kid, what am I going to do with you?" She told her that she had to love her. "I do at that. Every moment of every day. I think about all of you and love you to pieces."

The drive home was sprinkled with odd bits and pieces of conversation about what they'd been doing since Fred had died. Shipley hadn't realized that Amanda had sold her home and was living in something smaller. It suited her, the domestic part of her life. Not that she thought that she could stand idle but it seemed to be just fine for her sister.

They were about forty miles from home when they came up on a bad accident. It happened right in front of them, and Shipley was happy that they'd stopped for a break. They might well have been in the middle of it if not. Getting out of the car, she was racing towards the middle of things before she thought that she wasn't on duty right now with this sort of accident. By then, she came up on three cars that were smashed up under the back end of a semi. Barking orders, something that she thought she did a great deal, she was able to get several of the people standing around to get their asses in gear and help the wounded.

The man driving the last car was dead. She didn't even bother to check his pulse. She knew that when someone had their head removed, there was no coming back from that. The woman in the front seat was gone as well. The two kids in the back, one of them an infant was screaming their heads off. Getting them out of the car, it was her sister that took control of the little ones.

The second car had no survivors either. The two people in the front seat had both been killed when their car's airbags hadn't gone off. It was an older car, one of the show-off older kinds, so she doubted that they even had airbags like newer cars did. While she didn't know cars all that well, she knew that it had to have been before nineteen ninety-eight when they were mandatory in all cars built after that.

She didn't want to look in the first car. Shipley knew that no one could have survived the impact that took them at least five feet up and under the bed. Making her way to the car, careful of where she stepped, she was surprised as fuck when a little boy asked her if she was going to get him out of there.

"I know my grandma and grandpa are dead. I checked on them like I had seen them do on those doctor shows. Why do people check necks to see if they're alive or not?" She asked him his name and if he was hurt while she tried her best to pull the glass off the rear window where the kid was. Then she explained to him about the pulse. Mostly just talking while she took a good look at where the kid was. "Seth Morgan. I'm eleven. I saw that the truck had stopped and got myself on the floor. My grandma yelled at Grandpa to pay attention but it was too late by then. When he slammed on the brakes, I hit my head and woke up down here on the floor."

"How badly are you hurt?" He told her that his back was hurting. "Can you wiggle your toes? How about your head? Do you hurt there? I'm trying to get you out of here, but you're not in a good place right now."

"I can wiggle my body. I was trying my best to get myself off the floor when everything got quiet. And yeah, my head hurts. I got some blood on my face, but...well, I don't know if it's mine or my grandparents. They both are dead, right?" She told him that they were and had been nearly cut in half. "You didn't have to tell me that, you know."

"Sorry, Seth. I'm used to saying what needs to be said." She was able to get the glass out of the back window. She could see then that he was rammed between the seat he'd been in and the back of the seat from the front of the car. "I don't know that I can get you out without hurting you more. How about you and me just keep talking so that I can make sure that you're not too badly hurt?"

"I'm hurting now that I'm lying here." She told him that she didn't have anything to give him as she didn't have a medical bag. "I thought doctors were supposed to have them in their car at all times or something."

"I'm army, with a MASH unit." She then had to explain to him what that meant. Reaching into the car, she could just touch her hand to his head. Searching for any gapping wounds, she was satisfied that he didn't seem to have any large gashes nor much in the way of too much head trauma. "You've probably seen that show on television. If not, I'd highly recommend it as it's a funny show."

"You're talking to me on account of you not thinking that I'm going to make it, aren't you?" She said that she wouldn't do that to him, that she'd tell him straight up if she thought he was a goner. "Good. You're calming me down now, and that's good. But I'm feeling everything hurting, too. I surely wished that I could hold your hand. I'd feel a lot better if I could." He sobbed a little, and her heart went out for him.

"I'm going to hold onto your hand for as long as I can. I've only just noticed that I'm cut up badly on my arms, too. Not like you are hurt, but the pain is making itself known to me now. I'm sure that you know that feeling." He said that he knew. "All right, Seth, I can hear sirens now. Maybe it won't be too much longer."

"It seems like forever since I was jerked around under here. I guess I should be lucky that I didn't get killed, too. My dad, he's gone like my grandparents are." They talked off and on, the two of them. He told her that he was going to be sick just before he started throwing up. She asked him if he had any blood in his vomit, and he told her that it was too dark to see down there. "What do you think happened to me that made me sick? I'm not going to die, am I?"

"Not if I can help it. Stress can make you sick.

That's more than likely what it is. That's what I'm hoping for anyway." Someone behind her asked if she was all right. "I have an eleven year old male that I can't get out."

After telling the man that she was holding onto him and that he was sick to his stomach, he said that they were working on getting the semi to move up a little. He told her that she'd have to get off the car. The scream from Seth telling her not to leave him had her telling the man that she had a clearance that would keep her from being hurt when the trailer was moved upward.

It was another two hours before they got the semi to pull up. Then, it was an additional hour that they were able to get the little boy out. She was asked for her credentials, and once given, she was able to treat Seth when he was pulled free. Shipley was thrilled that the medical team working with her was able to allow her to give him some much-needed pain medication.

There was a chopper on site to get the survivors to the hospital. There were only the three that had been in the cars that were critical. A great many bumps and bruises that were taken by ambulance, and that was about it. It was then that she noticed that she was bleeding a little more than she'd first thought.

The team wasn't able to stitch her up. They had no clear way of knowing what was in the wounds, such as glass or something more. Shipley was taken away in the chopper when it returned for the second time. By then, she was completely exhausted and hurting. She could only hope that she didn't spend the next two weeks in the hospital. She had plans, damn it.

~*~

Locke was glad that he'd been called in to help out with the injured. So far, he'd stitched up forty-three people. There looked to him like there was no end to the people coming in for one thing or another. Since he was helping out, he kept an eye out for the person who had pulled a kid from the back seat of a demolished car. It was told to him that she'd been the first one on the scene and had been the one that had helped the medical and medical personnel that were out there as well. Heroes like that were well thought of, and he wanted to be the first to thank her for her help and service.

"She's being life-flighted in." He asked the nurse, her name was Brandy, if she'd been hurt.

"Something to do with glass is all I know. Her blood pressure is a little high, I was told, because she's upset that they brought her in with something that could get here quicker if there were more seriously injured people out there." Brandy started away, then stopped. "Oh, and she's army. Doctor with a MASH unit that's here for her sister or something."

He knew that Amanda had been on her way to pick up her sister from Columbus. It made him wonder if it could be the same person. Finishing up the elderly woman who had to have nineteen stitches in her arm, he asked her to please wait as it needed to be bandaged yet. She told him to hurry up. She had things to do today. Christ, would people ever be nice?

"She's in room fourteen, Locke. Be careful. I was told that she's spitting mad." He thought that he could handle someone's temper. His last two patients had been nightmares. As he opened the door to check on her. He was met with a police officer guarding her room.

"I'm here to assess her wounds. Then to stitch her up if necessary." She asked the other man what the fuck was he doing in her room. At least, he thought it was the other man. "I'm talking to you. Just give me a little something for the pain and take care of the others out there. I can stitch myself up. I've done it before."

He didn't have any doubt that she had either. There was something about the woman in army brown fatigues that told him not only was she pissed off, but she was going to be hard to nail down to help her out. Not that he minded. She was pretty to look at, and she had a beautiful temper.

"My name is Locke Erickson. I'm here to have a look at your wounds." She told him that she'd been looking at them all morning. "All right. I'm going to clean them out, with your permission, then I'll — "

She cut him off. "Listen, doc. I know that there are more patients out there than me. Just work on them, then I'll let you stitch me up. Also, take this jackass with you." He corrected her on both things. "Oh, then, Nurse Erickson, go ahead and do what you have to do. But if I hear that there were more people waiting to get their holes plugged up, I'm going to shoot you in the head."

The officer snickered, and Locke thought that Sergeant Shipley was going to come off the bed and do what she had threatened him with.

Also, he thought that their conversation escalated quickly but he didn't know her well enough to know if she was that volatile all the time or not. For some reason, it hit him that while she was pissed off, she wouldn't take it out on others that might be around her.

Cleaning her wound was made easier as she was able to move her arm, or he should say that she was cooperating by moving where he wanted her to. Not one for small talk, Locke decided that she wasn't either. Once he gave her pain meds, she did have a slight concussion on her head, that she laid back and seemed relaxed. He doubted that she was completely relaxed, however, knowing on some level that she was alert at all times.

"You do good stitches. Thanks. The last time someone put some in me, I had a fucking scar that never properly healed. It took me getting hurt again in the same place to have someone fix it." He told her that was his specialty. That and putting in IVs. "Yeah? Maybe I'll have you on my team. I'm betting that you'd just love it where I work."

"Doubtful that you do either." She asked him what he was talking about. "I don't know. Just a feeling that I have. You're Amanda's sister, aren't you?"

"I am. What can you tell me that she hasn't? Or won't, for that matter." He told her that he couldn't tell her anything other than his brother had helped her with the logistics of her getting everything ready so that she could get her insurance money. "I'm sure that he took his cut, too, didn't he? Everyone has their hands out when there is grieving to be done."

He finished up the stitches on both her arms and stepped back. When she grabbed his arm, something that he was sure she'd done plenty of times when dealing with the public, he stepped back further from her.

"I'm sorry. Not only was my comment uncalled for, but it was nasty. And I'm only nasty when I'm working. Or stressed. And I'm that twenty-four-seven." He said that it was all right. "No, it's not. It was, just as I said, rude, and I'm being a bitch. Tell your brother that I said thanks for taking care that no one else could take advantage of her. I think, and this is just between the two of us, but I never really cared for Fred, her husband. He allowed his mom to rule their married life, putting my sister through hell all the time. I'm profoundly sorry for my words and actions."

"Thank you." He asked her if she needed more pain medicines, and he gave her as much as he was allowed to. "Your sister is in the lobby. I'm to understand that she helped with a couple of kids while she was out there. Good for her. Amanda is a caring and compassionate person."

"Because I'm not, right?" He only raised a brow at her, and she apologized to him. Locke was sure that she wasn't used to doing that either. "I'll keep my mouth shut now. Thanks for doing a good job on my wounds. Do you know when I'm going to get out of here?"

"I don't, sorry. However, I can check on that for you." He glanced at the officer, who had his back to them, and watched the door. "What's he here for?"

"Don't know. He was in here when I was brought in. And he won't tell me dick." Locke asked the man why he was there. "Good luck with that. He seems to be one bit of cheese short of a cheese and cracker appetizer."

"My name is Officer Diller. I was told to, under no circumstances to allow anyone in here who was out to hurt her. I guess that came from

someone higher up on the food chain than I am."
Locke asked him if he knew who it had been. "No,
sir. Just that I was to protect her no matter how
much she bitched about it. I understand that now."

He made his way out to the lobby to find
Amanda. She and her daughter Mandy were
talking to a younger couple that had a newborn.
As soon as she saw him, she leapt up and wrapped
her arms around him. It felt really good after all
the stress of the day.

"I don't know if you can go back to see her
just yet. Another nurse came in to finish up her
dressings." She asked him what she'd done to need
to be in here. "I'm sorry, Amanda, I can't tell you
that. You understand. But she's getting the best of
care, and I can take you back. I want to warn you
that she's in a mood. I think myself that she's in a
mood like that all the time, but then I don't know
her."

"She is. Aunt Shipley doesn't like fools.
I'm not sure what that means, but she don't like
them." He asked Mandy if she wanted to hang out
in the nurses' station with him. "Nah. I want to see
my aunt, too. Momma said she's hard on people. I
don't know what that means either, but I love her

to specs and dust, I do."

Taking Amanda to her sister's room, he was glad to see that she wasn't being guarded by the police in her room any longer. However, two military cops were standing guard near the nurses' station now who looked like they would keep her safe at all costs.

"Oh, Aunt Shipley, look at your arms. Are you all right?" She told the little girl that she was but needed help in pulling her up to sit on the bed with her. Lifting Mandy up, she watched as the three of them were talking over one another and crying a little. Leaving them to their visit, Shipley called him back.

"I am sorry. I wanted to tell you how stupid I felt when you did not warrant my temper. But like you've heard from Amanda, I'm always pissed off." He told her that it was fine. "No, it's not fine. Why do people say that? I was rude, and I'm sorry. It's not anything but me saying I made a mistake by taking it out on you."

"Okay then. I'll see you later." He was still laughing a few hours later when he was on his way home. He'd never gotten such a disgruntled apology before. He had wanted to stick around and tell her it was fine again, but he didn't. Liking where his head and balls were right now. Besides, he and Alex, his wife, were trying to make a baby. There was no way that he was going to mess that up with her.

Dusty was in the driveway when he got home. After giving him a welcoming hug, he invited him into the house. Alex was there, he knew. He'd spoken to her about dinner tonight. They were going out, so he asked Dusty if he wanted to join them.

"Sure, I'd love that. But I have to run by the hospital really quick. I have someone there that is wanting to get information on changing their benefactor." He asked him if he knew who it was. "Not really. She's Amanda's sister, however. Did you get to see her today?"

"I did. She's banged up a bit. Nearly a hundred stitches, mostly to her right arm. I met her. Her name is Candace, like Amanda told us, but she goes by Shipley, her last name. She's someone in the service and they have two people there protecting her. Mostly from killing someone, I think. She has a temper that would rival the likes of Dad. But she doesn't use her fists. Just her words.

And she's quick to apologize when she feels like she's messed up too."

"Great. Just great on having to deal with her today. What is she, some debutant that thinks the world revolves around her?" Locke told him again that she was army. "I guess I wasn't paying attention. I'm going to run into town with you guys, and if you'll wait on me, we'll have a nice dinner. My treat."

They were all at the hospital about twenty minutes later. As his brother was headed to the emergency department, he and Alex sat in the lobby waiting on him. He heard the moment that he'd opened the door to her room. She was fired up again but this time not at him or his brother. Someone named Scott. He didn't catch the last name.

"You should probably go and save him. I'm betting right now that he volunteered to come here and help people with their final arrangements. Did someone die that she knew?" He said that he didn't ask her. She was in a shitty enough mood as it was. "Well, I'm going to go and help him. I'm very protective of my brothers."

The shrill whistle that he heard down the

hall where he was had him getting up and going to see his wife. He only knew one person that could do that and it was Alex. Hurrying faster when he heard someone cry out in pain, he was in the room just as he saw his brother have someone in a headlock. Alex was behind the bed, and Shipley was pointing her gun at his brother and the stranger.

He didn't know what to think about what was going on. Instead of thinking that things were Shipley's fault, he asked her what was going on. She looked at him as if she had no idea who he was.

"It's me, Nurse Erickson. I stitched you up." She didn't lower her gun but asked him to please get her something for pain. "I can do that for you. After you put down your weapon. You don't have to put it away. Just lower it away from my brother, please?"

"Get that jackass out of here." He started to reach for the other man when he asked him if he knew who he was. "I'm here to see Candy. She and I go way back, and she's just a little bit pissed off at me right now."

"He said he was here to marry me. Like

that's a good enough reason to come in here and propose to me. Again. Christ get him out of here before I have to double your job in putting him back together." The man, whatever his name was, said that he was serious. "I don't believe you. You waited until now to...Christ Scott, don't you see that I'm wounded here?"

"I do. That's the reason that I came here when I did. You'd be easier to talk to if you're recouping rather than doing surgery. Not that I'm going to allow you to do that once you tell me yes. My mother needs you to be around all the time now." She asked him if his mom knew what he was doing. "She's not a part of this. But yes. She told me that I had to get you to say yes to me. It's not like you have people chasing you down to ask you to be their wife, are they?"

Shipley snorted and asked him where her drugs were. "I think, too, I might have pulled out a few stitches while I was getting more upset with Scott."

Locke looked at the man that Dusty was holding onto and realized that he should know him. When Dusty released the other man, he knew in the next breath that the man was indeed very important. To this hospital, at least.

"Mr. Landry. I didn't know that it was you." Scott straightened up his tie and looked at him. "I'm sorry for this, but Shipley has been injured, and until a few minutes ago, I thought that she was headed home today."

"That's all right, Derick. She can be hard on some people." It was then that Shipley told the man that he was a moron and that his name was Locke. "Look, Candy. I just want you to consider us marrying. We're perfect for each other. You can retire now and be home with my mom and that will make the two of you closer than before."

"Your mother hates me. Not only that, but I've told you this before, I don't like her either. I have a job that I love. I'm not going to give that up to play nursemaid to your mom. She's a royal bitch, and you know it, and I'm not going to be giving her care unless it's some kind of doomsday drug that takes her out and your entire family." She narrowed her eyes at Scott. "Aren't you in violation of the court-ordered cease and desist that I have on you?"

"That's all water under the bridge now that you're back in the States. You shouldn't have done it in the first place, darling. I told you that the two of us just had a misunderstanding when you did that." Locke told the other man that he should leave and that he didn't want his patient upset any more than she already was. "She's just waiting for a bigger diamond, that's all. I know she's being all hard-assed, but she'll mellow out once we have children and my mom is happy."

"I don't think that she wants anything to do with you. Mellowing out or not." Dusty moved to stand in front of the gun that was still pointed at the man in charge of this hospital. "I don't know if you realize this or not, or perhaps it's larger than your brain can handle, but she has told you nicely — well, for her anyway, that she wants you out of here. Either do it, or I'll call the cops. A restraining order is in place, and while I'm not sure of the required feet you're supposed to stay from her, I'd say that you're in violation of it right now."

Dusty rolled his sleeves up, and that was when Shipley put her gun down. As soon as she did, Dusty popped the man in the face, one punch that had him falling to the floor and out cold. He was going to lose his job. He just knew it. Locke, however, didn't think he cared all that much. The man was a shithead, just like he'd heard that he was.

By the time the cops arrived, superseded by the two Army military police, he'd been able to take care of the broken stitches in Shipley's arms and have one of the doctors on the floor discharge her. He'd take her to his house if that's what it took for her to be safe or Landry to be safe. The fool.

Chapter 2

Dusty helped the woman out to the car that they'd all come in. He was getting a kick out of the way the MPs were treating the man who had come to the hospital. He was a pest, Alex told them when she mentioned the restraining order. She put her hands on her hips and asked them what the hell they were doing, not protecting someone in the care of her husband.

He surely did love a woman who had a fire in her eye as Alex had. The other woman, Shipley, looked about as hot, too. Dusty decided that he was going to enjoy working for the woman if only to see her temper flare. He wasn't foolish enough to get her going, nope. But he thought that he might enjoy watching her take a bite out of other people.

She was staying at Erickson Manor, and he was glad for that. Call him a sadist, but he was enjoying watching her take apart the two officers who had been assigned to protect her. The cop had some jurisdiction but not as much as the MPs who listened to her every command.

They didn't either one of them leave their posts right outside of the house when she was in here either. Her command of curse words that she had, in several languages if he didn't miss a beat, was profoundly entertaining.

"What are you grinning at?" He told her, point blank, what he thought of her and her temper. "You won't feel that good about me once I turn it on you."

"I'm not worried about that. I plan on being on my best behavior while around you." She made her way to the living room as soon as Dusty had her signing off on the last of the paperwork to make sure that her sister and her children benefited from her life insurance policy that she'd had since starting her career in the service. "Couldn't you have had this done by one of the men in the army with you? Not that I mind, really, but I was just curious."

"I'm on the front line all the time. Attorneys usually don't make it out to me when I need them."

He told her that he could understand that. "Don't you have someplace to be?"

"No. Locke and Alex invited me to dinner but with bringing you here, they've decided to go out and bring something back for all of us." She asked him what it would be, no doubt foo-foo food. "No. I don't even know what that is, but I think that they were talking Chinese when they left."

"From Woo Chow?" He said that it was where they usually got things to go. "I'd kill for a large bowl of their hot sour soup and a couple of dozen egg rolls."

Pulling out his phone, he asked Locke if they'd gotten their food yet. Telling him what Shipley wanted, he said that he'd get some. Then she asked for some green tea. He knew that Alex had a stash of it in the house, but he'd ask her. She told him that she did and would be happy to share.

Putting his phone away, he decided to get to know Shipley. First of all, he did wonder what her name was. When she told him that it was Candace and not Candy, he nodded once. Yes, she wasn't a Candy nor a Candace. He asked her what she wanted him to call her.

"Nothing. I'm not…it's not like we're going to be meeting up socially. Or for that matter at all. Just keep to yourself and we'll be just fine. I'm not here to be social but to help my sister out. She did tell me that your family did a great deal for her, and I can't thank you all enough for that." He leaned back on the couch and regarded her. "You're starting to piss me off. Didn't you just tell me that you weren't going to do that?"

"I'm not trying to piss you off. I was just thinking how much you look like Amanda yet I think I could tell the two of you apart. You're identical, I'm assuming." She said that she was the older of the two. Asking him what he found different about the two of them, as identical twins and he frowned before speaking. "Amanda is softer around the edges. I don't mean physically but just softer. Not that I don't think she could take care of herself as well as you do, but she's not one to fly off the handle when she's upset. Also, you have more freckles. Or she might cover them up with something. You have a natural look about you, while Amanda is more…I was going to say polished, but that wouldn't be right here. I think that given the right circumstances that you could outshine the sun."

"You're assuming a lot right now. And I never dress up." He asked her if she'd ever dressed up in her uniform. "Yes, for very special occasions and only something that I can't get out of. I've only been in my dress-up clothing, what I call people clothing twice in my career. Once when I was given a metal for something that I do for my job, and the second time was when I went to Amanda's wedding. She begged for me to wear it, and I couldn't turn her down. Besides, it kept Fred's mother in line, what with me being armed and all. Now there is what I'd call a first-class bitch."

They were still talking when his brother came home. Alex was on the phone, but his brother didn't seem to care that she wasn't helping him bring things in. As soon as Alex saw Shipley, she handed her phone off to her.

He left her to her call and joined Locke and Alex in the dining room sorting out food. There was a lot of it, too. He asked if they'd bought out the restaurant.

"No. I didn't know what Candace wanted so I got something of every dish. It's not like it will go to waste." He told her no, not if anyone else was coming. "Amanda and the kids are coming over too. That's who Candace is talking to. There was some mix-up about where she was staying, and I let her deal with that."

When Amanda arrived, Dusty could see the differences better. She didn't wear what he thought was called foundation, but she did have fewer freckles than Shipley did. He also wondered if it was because one spent more time in the sun than the other. And if Amanda had the time to do that, would she be as freckled as well.

The kids, even the infant, seemed to love their aunt. Especially Mandy. But the little boy, Fred, he would crawl up into her lap when he was upset more than he did his mom. Mom, he noticed, would tell him he was all right. However, Shipley would pretend that she was going to cut off the appendage or something along those lines, making the kids all laugh. A sudden thought occurred to him and he was dizzy with the thought of it being a reality.

He was just getting up to get something for the kids to drink when Shipley was coming out of the kitchen with her hands filled with juice glasses.

He saw her then. Saw Shipley when she was fat with a child. His child, and it made him have to sit down with his head between his knees.

"You all right, dumb ass?" He had to smile. Of course, she'd be no different with treating him than she was a child. "Sit up. You're scaring the shit out of the kids. You heard me. Sit your ass upright before I do it for you."

They were all eating once he was feeling better. Mandy sat down next to him and when she was ready for some more rice, he got it for her. After thanking him, she looked him right in the eyes. There was something about the look that startled him a little.

"Don't hurt her." He asked her what she meant. "My aunt Shipley. Don't hurt her. She's been hurt before. When she came home the last time, she was crying a lot. I don't know what it was, but she hurt really bad, and it hurt my heart because I couldn't fix it for her. She fixes me all the time, but I couldn't help her. So…please don't hurt my aunt."

"I won't. At least I'll try my very best not to hurt her." He didn't tell her that she looked as if she could take care of herself if he did, but he didn't. Something about the innocent request of a child had him trying his best not to be flippant to her. "Thank you for telling me about her last visit. Was it when your dad got sick?"

"No, that dumb grannie was upset that momma wasn't going to let her live in our house so that she could take care of her baby. She meant my daddy. Mom told me, and it hurt her that dumb grannie wouldn't allow her to do what was needed to care for Daddy. Then Aunt Shipley came home, and that was a fight, I tell you. But I could tell that she was sad too. I didn't know from what, but she and Momma cried all night that night, and she was gone the next day. She flew in for a quickie visit she told us."

"That was good that she could drop everything and come to your momma's aide, don't you think? I mean, that might have been all that it was. She was sad for her sister." Mandy assured him that it wasn't just that. But then Fred wanted to go and play, and she left the table with him.

"Don't be getting ideas that you can charm something out of my family." He looked at Shipley and asked her what she meant. "I don't know, but you'll not hurt the kids to do something to me.

Come right out with what you're asking me, and I'll tell you."

"She was telling me about her dumb grannie—I have a feeling that she calls her that all the time, not just now. But she was telling me how when your brother-in-law first got sick, she wanted to move in with them to take care of her baby. I believe it hurt her that she didn't mean the kids for their mom." Shipley nodded and said that was true. "Then she told me that you came home and that you and your sister cried all night, then you left her. I don't think that she minded so much that you were there over Grannie, but she did hurt when you left. She didn't say that, but it was in the way that she told me that you were gone the next morning."

"I had a deadline to meet. I did leave without being able to tell her bye. I'll not do that again. Thank you for telling me that." He asked her why she was crying. "You don't know me well enough to ask me about that. Maybe someday, but not now."

"I'll tell you something that I've told very few people other than my family. I have a friend that I care for. Her name is Lila Sheppard. I was supposed to be her date for the prom when we first moved here. I was all set to do it, but the school didn't like the fact that I was nearly twenty years old and too old to be with an eighteen-year-old girl." She asked him what happened to her. "The boy that took her to the prom beat the shit out of her and raped her. She lives in a state of limbo now, not talking or responding to her family. I take care that she's getting the best of care even though I can't see her. Her parents have no idea that I'm the one who is paying for her nursing home." He gave himself a good hard shake. "I don't know why I told you that. As I said, I've never told anyone that but my brothers."

"Thank you for sharing it. I won't say a word to anyone either. You're a very kind man, and I'm glad that my sister has you and your family in her corner." He thanked her. "No problem. But I need to stretch myself out."

They were sitting on the back veranda when she got up to walk in the yard. It was much too large to be called a porch, and the things that were back there made it seem as if it were a part of the house rather than something you sat on to get a cool breeze in the evening.

There were fans that were on all the time but for winter. A small ice box, one that had seen better days that was forever filled with bottled water. And there were several fruit trees right off of it that you could reach out and get a few plums or apples should you wish. And in the early spring, the place was alive with blooms and flowers.

He watched Shipley play with the children. She was good with them, not overly harsh when she spoke to them. Dusty had a thought that she'd make a good mom, but she'd be a little overly protective of them. Then he laughed at himself. She'd be as overly protective of them as he thought that he would be.

It was getting late, and the kids wanted to go to bed. Helping carry them out to her car, Amanda cornered him. She asked him what his intentions were with her sister. It took him several seconds before he could form an answer.

"I have no intentions of hurting her. If that's what you mean." She said that she honestly didn't know what she meant but saw the way that he looked at her. "Like what, if you don't mind me asking you."

"Like you're the big bad wolf, and she's little

Red Riding Hood." He laughed. Actually threw back his head and laughed. "Are you laughing at me?"

"No. Not at all. I was just thinking that I'd be the little girl, and your sister would be the wolf. I'm just a man who'd like to see your sister in another way than when she's hurt or upset. However, I have a feeling that she'd be upset about something all the time. Would that be correct?" She told him that she didn't know. That she missed so much of her life. "I'm sorry about that as well, Amanda. I don't know what I'd do if I didn't have my brothers right there for me all the time. I'd miss them so much."

"I miss her as well. But she has this sixth sense about when to call me. I think that it's a twin thing. But she'll just call me out of the blue, and that'll make me feel better." He told her that he was glad that they were so close. "We are. More than I think any other twins that I know of."

"She said that she's only home for a few weeks now. Is that right?" She said that she had four weeks, but one of them had been getting better. "All right. We'll have a good time while she's here, and you can reap all the love that you can while she's visiting. I have a feeling that she's missing you as well."

"Good. Maybe when she retires, she can buy herself a little home and be close to me again. What do you think?" He said that he had no opinion on that as he didn't know either of them very well. "Well, get on the stick, Dusty. She only has three weeks left of her vacation."

She kissed him on the cheek and got into the car. It looked to him like all four of the people in the car were asleep, including Shipley. He wondered if he'd call Shipley that all the time when...he let that thought go and decided that he was going to let things go for now and make sure that Amanda and her sister had as much time together as they could get.

~*~

Shipley missed the banter that she'd had with Dusty. He was funny at times and an irritant the other times. But she liked him. And that, she realized, was something that she didn't much care for. Just as she was going out to her car, she was running errands for her sister when she saw Scott standing next to her car.

"I've come to propose to you, Candy. And I

do hope that you'll realize that I've put a great deal of thought into this. You're going to have to retire, however. My mother isn't too keen on you living with us but she'll come around once she sees you for what you are. You're going to be able to take care of her in ways that she told me about." She asked him what that was supposed to mean. "That you're a mushy person and that you put on this façade of being bad assed in order to keep me at bay. I don't much care for you seeing that Derick person either."

Just as she was ready to pull out her gun and end her trouble with Scott, Dusty pulled into the drive and got out of his truck. However, he didn't so much as come to her defense but seemed to be letting her handle things.

She had no idea why, but she really liked him for that. She wasn't going to use the 'L' word. Shipley had been telling herself that she wasn't in love with the moron for the last several days. Walking to him, he stood up straighter, and she pulled his face to hers and kissed him.

He hesitated for just a second, and she started to pull away, feeling foolish for doing this to a near stranger. But he wrapped his arms around her and pulled her closer to his body and deepened the kiss to the point of her needing to strip him down and take him right there on the hood of his truck.

Gently, he pulled away from her, not, however, letting her go. She could see the lust in his eyes and she knew that he was seeing the same in hers. Turning in his arms, barely able to stand on her own, she looked at Scott. The look on his face was priceless and she was glad that he might well be getting it through his thick head that she wasn't going to be marrying him. Ever, if not longer.

"What is the meaning of this?" Scott stomped his way to her and got down on one knee. "I've gotten you a ring. Though with your showing off right now, I don't know why I don't get you something smaller. But momma said that if I was going to do this, then I might as well go big. I got you the biggest ring. It's not a diamond, I'm not spending that kind of cash on you just yet but it's the biggest looking diamond that I could find."

Dusty turned her around and looked into her eyes. She could see that he had a strange look on his face, and while she'd not known him all that long, she knew that it wasn't going to bode well for Scott.

"You're not a diamond person, are you?" She shook her head, wondering how he knew that. "I have a ring for you as well. It's perfect for you. It belonged to the greatest woman that I knew, right up until you came into my life. If you would consent to saying yes that you'll marry me, I'll slip it on your finger right now."

"You have it on you?" He nodded, pulled away from her long enough to reach into his car, and put a small blue box in her hand. "You have to do it right. Will you?"

"Yes." He moved back again but didn't let her go. Getting down on both his knees he took the box back and kissed her hand before opening the box. "Candace Lynne Shipley, will you consent to being my wife? Allow me to pamper you when you need it? Your sounding board when you need that, too. I will follow you to the ends of the earth, either on this soil or wherever your job takes you. I have fallen in love with you so quickly that it took my mind longer to figure out what my heart already knew. I'm so deeply in love with you."

"There are no takebacks, Dusty. You get that, right?" Scott interrupted them and said that he'd asked first. Shipley turned to him. "Shut up, you idiot. This wasn't a contest or a game that you can play. This is forever. This is love." She looked at him again. "Right?"

"Yes, no contest, no game. Yes, I want you to marry me forever and a day. Forever be my wife. I'd also like to have children if you're willing to do—" Scott cut him off.

"There will be no children. Never. I don't like them, and I hate the way that they smell. No, I refuse to allow you to have any children." She looked at Scott while he spouted off his demands, and he could tell that he was seriously thinking that she'd not have children if she wanted them. "You should take me more seriously, Candy. I swear, if you don't, then things might happen to your lovely little family."

"Did you just threaten her?" He kissed her hand and then stood up, but not before slipping the ring on her finger. "Did you just threaten my future wife? And our families?"

"I don't know that I'd call it a threat but more like a promise. It would be a big shame that your brother would suddenly lose his job. And that I'd have to make sure that the hospital never treats anyone in your family again. Momma told me to tell you that. While I'm not sure how I could make that happen, I want you to know that I will do whatever my momma tells me to do." Scott smiled at them. It was evil-looking. Pure evil. "Yes, a right shame if one of those little kiddies that your sister has was to fall ill and have to be taken to a bigger city with less new equipment to—who are you calling now?"

She wanted to know that as well. But when he started talking, she was never so proud of anyone as she was at this moment. He called his brother to tell him what was going on.

While she had no idea what was being said on the other end of the call, she was happy when he said that Shipley had consented to marrying him. Then he went on about how Scott Landry had threatened them. Kissing her quickly on the mouth, her sister came out to see what was going on.

"He's asked me to marry him. And dumb fuck here just threatened you and your kids with not getting any care if you're ever hurt." She hadn't any idea what she had expected her sister to do, but she couldn't be happier.

The punch to Scott's face not only knocked

the man back, but it also knocked him out. The silence was golden as she so often heard during her life. The police were pulling into the drive about the time that Locke showed up with his wife. If she didn't know better, she'd swear that the troops were called in, and there was going to be a lot of shit hitting the fan tonight.

Locke and his brother left after all of them showed up and left their cars in the drive. Within minutes, they were back and kissing her on the cheek to tell her congratulations. Then the idiots left again. Someone said they were headed to the bank. Whatever that meant.

Scott was taken away, and the officers looked at her sister's hand to make sure that she didn't need medical help. The two officers who had been to the house before when Scott had shown up also kissed her on the cheek, welcoming her to the Erickson family, and left with Scott. They didn't even check his wound, even though he had bitched about the pain he was in for so long. After they all left, all of them leaving with her and her sister promising not to leave, the two of them sat on the first porch and waited for them to return.

"Is it a lovely ring, Candace? Please don't

make me beg to see it." They both laughed, and she got her first look at the ring. "It's the same color as our eyes. Do you suppose that he picked it for that? Amethyst are about the closest thing that I've ever seen to judge our eye color." She told her sister that he'd come here with it. "I don't suppose he told you why he was coming here in the first place?"

"No. But he didn't butt in when Scott was spouting off his mouth about the rules when I marry him. He said that he wanted to have kids but would leave the decision up to me. I never thought about having them before, but now that's all I can think about." Amanda asked her about her job. "I don't know what to do about that. I want to retire, I told you that but I only have six months until I can retire with all my benefits. That's not a long time, is it?" She told her no, it wasn't if they had the rest of their lives together. "I'll talk to…I never thought that I'd think that I'd have to talk about myself and what I'm doing with anyone before. It's kind of a heady thing. Did you and Fred talk all the time?"

"Rarely. I mean, I suppose we talked about things…Can I tell you something? Something I'm only just figuring out." She told her sister that she could tell her anything. "I don't know that I ever loved Fred. Not the way I think that I should have. I see the love you have for Dusty, and I think the world would know that you love him, but it's also the way that Locke talks to Alex. The way they talk to each other. From the beginning, it was more arguments than anything between Fred and me. Then I got pregnant with Mandy, and it was sort of like we had to get married. I don't know that I'd do that today if I knew what real love was like."

"That's really sad, don't you think?" She nodded, then shook her head. "What do you mean? You would have done it all over. You just told me that you'd not."

"I'd not have Parker and Fred if I hadn't stayed with him. And they were worth every second of the things that I had to endure. That's sad, too. I had to endure my marriage to someone else. But I'm not going to think about that. I'm going to get on with my life. Perhaps date a little and move on. I have my health, my kids, and a good bit of money in the bank. Also, I have you and the Erickson family. They're a good group to have on your side if you were to ask me."

The house phone was ringing when they

stepped into the house. It was the police and they wanted to talk to her. Taking the phone from her sister, she said her last name and asked what she could do for them.

"Did you at any time pull out your weapon and aim it at Mr. Landry? He said that you threatened him, and that was why he said what he said in the heat of the moment." She told him what happened and then said that her sister had cameras all around the house, and it had sound if he wanted to hear it. "No, that's all right. I just wanted to ask you. I would have shot him myself, but then he's not saying anything to us. By the way, he is saying that he asked you to marry him first and that you did him dirty. But when Dusty asked you, you had an answer. Congratulations on that. He's a great man. By the way, Scott said that he's going to sue you for that. Just a heads up."

"Thanks. He did ask first." She relayed what he'd said about children as well as how he wasn't buying her a diamond. "I didn't even want a diamond. The ring that I got from Dusty is so much more wonderful than a diamond. He said that I wasn't...I have no idea why I'm telling you this."

"You're a friend, that's why." He cleared his throat. "I was wondering something. And you can tell me to fuck off or not. But when do you think that your sister will be ready to date again? I know that I sound insane for asking you that, but I've had a major thing about your sister since before she married Fred. He was a good guy and all but I don't think he treated her all that well. I'm sorry if you think that I'm out of line."

"You're not. And I'd say…give her a month. If she doesn't ask you out, then you ask her. I think that the two of you would make a good couple. I think that she's not really into getting married or anything but she might date you for a little bit. However, remember, I'm never too far away to make you pay if you hurt her or one of her children." He said he'd never hurt any of them. "Good. Then you have my blessings to ask her out."

Chapter 3

Dusty was on the board of trustees of the hospital. He hadn't really wanted to be. It just happened that way. When Martha, the woman that they all had fallen in love with when moving here, when she would ask them to do something, they did it for her. She had always steered them in the right direction, and even in death, they still thought of her to do things that would keep making her proud of them.

She would have told him to fire Scott several months ago had she still been with them. The man was insane to think that someone who loathed him as much as Shipley did would marry him. He looked around the table of the men and women that were on the board as well. When asked if he had anything to say, he stood up.

"As you all know, my family has been

taking care of this hospital since we moved here. Donating not just our hard-earned money but also our time and efforts to keep things well running here. But the funding will stop if you continue to keep Scott Landry on as an employee. This is the first time that we've had any interaction with you to do something that we want, and after all this time, it's something that needs to be done before he gives the hospital a bad name." He named off all the things that they'd been able to find out about the man in the short amount of time that they had.

Fifteen minutes before the board was called together, his family was able to find nearly thirty things that the man had been reprimanded on, written up about, and talked to about his behavior. That was a lot of things to have on your record for only the first five days of the month.

"My family has mentioned four times before that Scott Landry is a problem here, and according to the notebook that I have from his office, he's been doing things behind the back of all of us that should have been picked up on sooner than this." They asked him what kind of things that they supposedly had on the man. "I have it right here."

He handed each of them a copy of the pages

that he'd only been able to glance at when Alex had told him what to copy. In addition to the things in the book that involved the hospital, there were things in the book that had to do with not just Shipley but her sister and her husband as well. He had the staff hold pain meds from the man that might have made him rest easier. They certainly would have made his death a bit more comfortable than it had been.

The men and women of the board were reading over the papers as he finished up handing them out. There were several questions, which he had expected, but there were also a lot of them saying that they had had trouble with him as well.

"I don't want to tell you what to do. But if he continues to work here, you'll find the funding that we donate here taken off our books. As it stands right now, we have stopped payments made to keep the nursing staff in things that they need to get their jobs done. Also, the wing that is being funded by the Martha Grable foundations, which my brother oversees, will stop as well." One of the women asked him if he was blackmailing him. "Call it what you wish, but would you keep a man on that you can see for yourself is causing trouble over the hundreds of thousands of dollars my family donates to you yearly?"

Gathering up his things, he was on his way down the elevator when he heard from the board. They had decided to fire Scott. However, they weren't pleased about the blackmail of their funding. As soon as he saw Locke and the other, he was going to tell them to stop donating money to the hospital by half. He didn't like the way that he'd had to do what he'd done either.

He was glad to see that they had done as they said on his way out of the hospital. Much to his surprise they were calling in the police in the event that something went wrong. While he didn't think that the man was the violent type, he was single-minded and would drive them crazy with his way of thinking things through. Watching the men gather with the others made him feel good about having to put his foot down. He also didn't care to be doing that as it made him feel like he was making demands on the staff that he'd been trying his best to make sure had all that they needed to work.

Dusty was headed home when he heard from Shipley. She told him that she was at his house and had some questions for him. Diverting himself to his home, she was standing on the front porch when he pulled into his driveway. Then he corrected himself. It was their driveway now.

"Why on earth did you buy such a huge assed house?" He laughed, telling her what Martha, the woman that they compared all women to, had told him all the time about going big or going home. "I suppose that's about as good a reason as any; however, if you think that I'm filling these rooms with babies, then you have to rethink that. I'm not a broodmare."

"No, you are not." He kissed her on the mouth. "What was it that you wanted to ask me? I'm in a sore mood. Not bad; I just think that the hospital board hurt my feelings. Whiney? Yes, but they should have taken care of the man long before now."

"I agree. Okay. You have eleven bedrooms if you count the playroom on the third floor. I've been in all of them and if you ask me, there needs to be something done to the ones on the upper floor. The rooms are much too small to be anything but for an office or storage." He asked her what she had in mind. "Well, and you can tell me no if you wish, but what if there were only two bedrooms on that floor, and we take the middle one and make it a part of the master bedroom. The other one can be an office, that's about all it's going to be good for that people can't just wander into our private area and then have a bedroom worthy of a house this large." He asked her about the other bedrooms.

"There are eight of them down the long hall. Four on either side of it. While I do know that they're a good size for a bedroom for kids, just putting that out there, I think that only having the one bathroom at the end of the hall will cause trouble when we have daughters. I hope that they're just like you, by the way." She glared at him. "Or sons. I could care less so long as we can make them be good people that we can be proud of."

"While you're right about the bathrooms, I can't think of a way to make that happen without tearing up the entire house to get it done." He kissed her again, loving how it made her look frustrated when she was asking him something.

"Will you stop that and pay attention to me? I'm trying to be serious here. If we start having sex, I want to be prepared for any child that might come from it. And yes, before you ask, I'd be thrilled to have a child with you. But I want this taken care of first. What do you say?"

"I say that we have August come in and look around. I think he has a minor in architecture that has come in handy a few times. I know that he loves doing it but starting out, it didn't make him as much money as he thought that they should be making. I don't know what that means to him. But call him, tell him what we were thinking, and let him guide us to make it so that we have the least amount of mess that we can have." She asked how come he didn't do that for a living now. "I don't know. I believe that he has his reasons but I can't for the life of me remember if he told me about it or not. He is really good at facts, so that might be it."

She was calling his brother when he went into the first bedroom on the second floor. Shipley was right. They were about big enough for a bedroom but not much more. This particular bedroom had a full-sized bed in it that he'd picked up somewhere a while ago. For a time, he'd been using the bed but now he slept on the first floor. There was a nice-sized room down there that he was sure was supposed to be like a gaming room but he liked the way that the sun shone into the room on a sunny day.

"He's coming over now. Demitrius is coming with him. There is a job opening up someplace that he wants to talk to you about." Shipley looked at him. "Why do you work? I know you're supposed to have a ton of money, so why not...you know what? I've answered that for myself. You'd never be the type of person that would just be idle. I'm betting, too, that you make all kinds of money for yourself and your family, too, don't you? How did you start out with all this money? I don't know why, but I have a feeling that you didn't come from money."

"We didn't. And that's a good story. When we were all living at home with our father, an abusive man that we hated with every breath that we took. We'd play the lottery. Not all of us, but mostly, it would be Locke. He would play all our birthdays and since Demitrus and Knox were born on the twenty-third of a month, he used that second number to use as the power ball doubler. It's been about twelve years since we won, and the amount, a staggering fifty-six billion that we didn't have to share with anyone, has about doubled since then. Or more, I guess, if you count the money that Locke has from Alma's estate. Which he shared with us as well." She asked him if he was serious. "Yes. Forever serious when it comes to money. If we were to separate out our own money from working, I'd have the most as I sometimes invest in things that the family doesn't want to. I've taken chances that they didn't want to for one reason or another and have done very well."

"You're a billionaire. The six of you are billionaires. Is that what you're saying?" He smiled at her and nodded. "I'm going to need words here, Dusty. You're all billionaires, and you've never, I'm assuming, that you've never told anyone, and that's why no one believes you when you say things like you did today with the board."

"Pretty much. The banker here in town wouldn't allow us to open an account with them when we first moved here. As you might well understand, we left with literally nothing but the clothing on our backs. We left behind everything, not taking even a picture for fear of our father or someone would find us. I believe to this day that's the only thing that saved us." She asked him about his father. "I know that he died sometime back.

Not that any of us went to his funeral or even paid for it, though we could have. As I said, he was an abusive bastard that knocked us around more than necessary. Our mom, for all we know, could be dead as well. She left us when we were little to save herself from our father. The older I got, the more selfish I realized that she was. We didn't contact her either, even though we had enough money to do so. I don't know, however, if she's gone but I'm assuming so. If she is still alive, she'd be in her late eighties by now. I don't know for sure."

She sat there on the couch with him. A couch like the bedroom set that he had in one of the spare bedrooms was used and looked pensive. When she stood up, putting out her hand, he took it into his.

"This house is lacking in even the basic needs here. We have no bedroom furniture but for a mattress laying on the floor. Four plates, three forks, and one glass that we have to share. We're not going to go crazy with your money—" He corrected her. "All right, our money, but we need to get this house in some kind of finished state. We'll talk to August, then go to town. I'm the type of person who likes to test things before buying them. So, no internet buying. All right with you?

Also, I'll sign a prenup if you wish."

"I don't want that. What I have is yours now." He pulled out his wallet and thought it funny that he only had four one dollar bills in it. But a lot of credit cards. "We can use these or not. I don't know where they came from other than they had my name on them, and...Alex told me not to cancel them as they'll ding my credit score. Which is really good, she told me."

He told her how Alex had gotten them to look at their credit. How people were charging them for things that they didn't need. Then he told her how he was paying several cable bills for the same house and that Locke had been paying for someone to come into his home and press his suits. That he didn't wear but once in a while.

"What am I going to do with you, Dusty? You're a brilliant man who has no idea what kind of credit score you have." She looked at the credit cards in his wallet. "These are all for specialty stores. We'll use the credit card that is taken everywhere so that we don't have to pay so much in interest. Also, we'll have dinner. I don't want to make you broke so we're going to keep a running total of what we spend for each room."

August showed up about the time they had decided where they were headed. However once August started looking around, they were going to have to go tomorrow. He had ideas about the bedroom that they both loved. It was something that he'd done in his own home recently.

"More than likely, six bedrooms will be plenty. Just cut the middle one out and add bathrooms to all of them, even if they have to be like a Jack and Jill bathroom—though now that I think about it might not work. Just put a bathroom in each bedroom, and it will make everyone happy. Larger rooms, too." They agreed with him. "I can have a crew up here as early as Monday. Also someone to come in and redo the upper levels as well. I think that's what Locke and Alex are doing to the nursey that they uncovered, too."

~*~

Scott was so pissed off that he had a headache from it. How dare Candy turn him down when he'd asked her first. Not to mention turning to that fool Derick or whatever his name was when he was standing right there with his ring out.

Of course, the bastard had a ring, too. But he'd bet anything that it was a fake diamond or something equally stupid. Like one he'd gotten from a bubble gum machine. The man was so uncouth that he wanted to smack him around every time he saw him. They were stupid with their money, too. His momma had told him that information just yesterday when she'd come to talk to him.

They'd used Ms. Garble's money to renovate that big ugly house on Main Street. And he knew for a fact that the men did not have a dime between them when they'd come into town either. His brother had been the banker for the local one when they'd come here. Not once did they come into the place to open an account.

Barry had been the bank manager for a decade when suddenly he was pulled out by the police one morning and arrested. They said that he was skimming money off of the bank's end of day. If he'd told his brother once, he'd told him a million times, don't piss where you took a nap. He'd also told him not to get caught. That was what his momma had taught the two of them since they were little men. The police didn't care for people to be messing with the bank funds. That's the reason that he was in the hospital working. There were no funds there but a lot of people's lives that he could fuck around with. And he did. Everyday.

But the Erickson's took the check that Alma, the old woman that they'd cuddled up to when she got hers, they'd come in and put it into her account. Not cash it out like he would have done and pocketed the money. Nope, the idiots had left it in her account for her to pay her bills.

Scott thought that when you got to a certain age, they should be doubling up on their bills. Charge them twice for whatever they had in the way of utilities. It was a certainty that they'd not be around long, so why not get as much out of them as one could. They just never thought like he did when it came to old people. Speaking of which...

When he heard wheezing coming down the hallway to the cell he was in, he knew that it was his momma. When she got to the place he'd been put in, she banged on his cell bars and told him to come closer so that she could knock him around. Of course, he didn't. There was no way that he was going to be letting her beat on him while in jail.

A chair was brought for her, and her oxygen tank was sat up close to her. She was forever totting around a large tank so that she could continue breathing. She sat down with a huff and the chair actually spread its legs out wider, like it understood it was in danger with her sitting in it.

"Well?" He asked her what she meant. "Well, did she tell you no like I told you she would? I have told you and told you what to do with her. Grab her off the streets and knock her around a bit. Then tell everyone that you had her so that she'll be spoiled for other men. Did you do that?"

"No. She carries a gun. I told you that, too. I think that she'd shoot me before I could get her to listen to me." His momma told him that he was a fool then. "Do you really think that I'd be able to get her to listen to me? She doesn't seem to listen to anyone that talks to her."

"That's why you gotta show her who the boss is. Dang it, Scott, I told you that she needs to be caring for me in my olden age. With her being a doctor, she'll not be able to charge me those big prices to keep me alive. You can't do it and have a job. She can lift me up. She's got them strong arms from being in the army. I need her to be around so that I can show her how to be a good daughter-in-law, too. What are you waiting on?" He told his momma what had happened at the house when he'd been arrested. "So what? That man didn't ask her first. She's bonded to you now. You tell her that she has to marry you now on account'a you having asked her first. We should have thought of that before. You binding her with you by asking."

"I don't know that I want to be married to her. She's a real mean person, momma. Is there anyone else that you can think of that will be able to move you around? I think that I'd be better off leaving her alone. She carries that gun, too, and has men around her all the time, so she's protected. I told you that." Momma told him to stop being a pussy and to listen to her. "I have been, and so far, all I've gotten is a headache when her sister hit me."

"Her sister hit you? Well Jeeze Louise, Scott, how do you think that's going to sound when it gets around? People already don't have much in the way of respect for you. This is going to make you a laughing stock." He told her that he knew that, too. "Did you at least hit her back? I would have."

"I couldn't. I got knocked out." She didn't take too kindly to that information either. When the door opened down the hall, they both waited to see what was coming. He hoped it was another person to be in jail. It was lonely not having anyone to talk to all day. That's why the hospital job was so good for him.

He could walk around like he was in charge. He was, to a point, in his mind anyway. Just the nurses were in his department. However, he did try to manage the doctors too. But they knew he was lying when he said he'd been in charge of them. They'd just go about their business as if he'd ever said a word to them. Damned upstarts, as his momma would call them.

"Mr. Landry? I have a message from the hospital for you." He reached for the sheet of paper, but his momma snatched it away before he could get it. "It says you have been fired. My sister works there. She told me that you were a bully to everyone. I'm glad you lost your job."

The man walked away, laughing his fool ass off. He had to wait until his momma got finished with the note before he could read what their excuse was for firing the best man they had. She crumbled the note up and tossed it in the hallway.

"They said that you've been fired so that the Ericksons don't take back their funding. What does that mean?" He told her that he honestly didn't know that the Ericksons had any money. Then he told her what his brother would say to him. "So they have enough to have something to do with the new wing it said. The only new part of that hospital had been from Martha…what was her last name? Grable, that's it. And since it was in her name, then that means that they had nothing to do with it but to spend that old woman's money when her son was left out in the cold. Did you know that? She didn't leave her son a single dime. That's not right. Even gave her house to that nurse, Derick or something. The one that you're forever telling me about."

He'd heard that story, too. That the six men had pulled up in a van, and when it broke down, they went into the house and started making it their own. Not the real story, but that was the one he liked better than them helping out old Lady Grable so much that the house became a showcase and was featured in all kinds of magazines. And that Locke—another stupid name for a person— had gone to nursing school to become a good nurse to take care of the old broad in her later years. Christ, it sickened him when he thought of what a waste of time it had been to keep that woman hanging around longer than her time. He wished someone would take out his momma at times. She could be as mean as a rattler when she wanted to.

"You've lost your job. Now you need to get married to that girl. Fast too. I'm not going to keep you with my social security, either. That's barely enough for me to get my medications and my hair done once a week. You tell her that I said to get her bottom in gear and say yes. Then, if that don't work, you tell her that I'm coming for her if she don't. I'm finished with that girl putting you off all the time." He told her that he'd have to get out of jail first. "I'm making arrangements for that to happen too. I can't believe that they're making me, of all people, have to bail you out. What do they think that I'm made of? Money? Certainly not."

There was quite a kerfuffle when his momma had asked for a senior discount on his bail. He didn't know what that would have entailed with her, but he was sure that she should have been given it. She was almost sixty-five, so that should count for something, he thought. But then he realized that he'd not have given her a discount either if she'd been in his hospital.

When he got out, he made his way to the hospital. He had something to do there, and most importantly, he was going to make them give him his job back. There was no reason whatsoever that he should be out of work because of the Erickson people. What had they ever done for the hospital, he wondered.

The security team was called as soon as he came in the front entrance. The lady at the reception desk told him that he wasn't to be there. Like anything would get done if he wasn't. Leaving her there to go and deal with his office, he made his way to the elevators to go up to his floor.

His badge wouldn't work in getting him into his office. The dammed people took forever to get him his overtime pay when he had it, but they were Johnny on the spot to turn off his badge when they supposedly fired him. It wasn't until security chased him all over the hospital before finding him that he could get one of them to open his door. And even then, they told him that he didn't work here and they'd not do it.

After explaining to them how Derrick was to blame for the misunderstanding, he told them that he had to get out his book if nothing else.

It was what he wrote about in it that kept him informed. Like which two people were having an affair. Which nurses had the best ass. The one that had the biggest breasts, too. There were notes on everyone, and he'd use it against them all if they didn't let him do his flipping job.

"You're not going in there or anywhere else in the hospital, Mr. Landry. You're to leave now. Before we call the police and have you taken back to jail." He said that he'd only just been free of there. "Be that as it may. If you don't leave now, we're going to make sure that you stay put this time. I'm not kidding you when I tell you that the police won't be as nice to you as we've been."

"You haven't been nice to me at all. You're trying to kick me off the premises like I have no right to be here. I'm in charge of the nursing department." He said that he wasn't, actually. "As I have said to you twice now, there was a simple misunderstanding that I'm going to clear up soon. I just have to get into *my* office and get *my* book."

The police were called and he still hadn't gotten into his office. He couldn't even get the daily schedule that he had himself on. It was to make sure that he hit one part of the hospital daily.

These people were not cooperating with him, and now he was headed back to the flipping jail.

This time, there was no bail that could be paid. When his momma couldn't pay it, he'd already tapped her out she'd told him he tried calling Candy. Surely, she'd come to help him. He'd have to threaten her, too, if she didn't. There wasn't any way that she was going to leave the love of her life in jail to rot.

"I need to call Candy." None of the officers knew who he was speaking about. "Candy Shipley. Of course, you know who she is. We're getting married soon."

"I don't think you have the right of that, Mr. Landry. She's set to marry Dusty." He asked who that was. "You call him Derrick all the time. In fact it's been brought to my attention that you call everyone that you don't know Derrick. Even the women. That's very sloppy work on you if you really do that."

"I don't have time to learn people's names. I have enough going on with my momma and that errant soon-to-be wife of mine." He was told that Shipley—who he had to have explained to him who she was—wanted nothing to do with him. "Well, that's just too bad on her part. I want you to call her up right now and tell her that I'm demanding her to get her bottom here and bail me out so that we can talk wedding plans."

While he was being escorted out of the hospital, all he could think about was why he was so obsessed with marrying a woman that he didn't particularly like all that much. She'd never been nice to him. Not even when they were in school together. She was forever treating him like he was a pest, like a fly buzzing around her head and nothing more. So why did he want her? He asked himself again and again. What the hell was wrong with him? That was something else that he asked himself times a day and still had no answer.

Chapter 4

Going back to work today, Shipley wasn't thrilled. First, because she was on desk duty, something that she hated more than anything, and secondly, she was having to fill out reports for the reason for her having to be on sick leave. However, she was very proud of the things that she'd gotten done for her sister and her new home that she would share with Dusty.

"There's a call for you on line two." Picking up the phone, she was still reading the report's information when she said hello. When no one spoke, she said her name and rank and asked who was there. She knew immediately it was Scott when he asked her where she was.

"I'm working. What are you doing?" He asked her why she was working. "Because I have a job. Why are you asking me questions that are none of your business? I have shit to do, and you're not helping me get shit done."

"I want to talk to you." She told him to talk. "Can I come to you? I don't want my momma to hear me. She's got herself spies everywhere, and I don't want her to be pissed off at me while I'm speaking to you."

"I'm in DC. Are you even close to me?" He asked her again what she was doing working. "We are not going over this again. Tell me what you want to say then get off the phone. I have two stacks of paperwork here that I have to get finished up before I can get my ass home."

"Do you have…never mind. You won't tell me. I don't want to be married to you." She started to be flippant with him, telling him that she didn't want to be married to him either when he spoke again. "Momma wants it on account of you being strong and a doctor. I don't want to be married to anyone that is stronger than me. She's making me do all kinds of things that she thinks will make us have to get married. Also, I don't think that she gets around like some people. She thinks, first of all, that I can simply knock you around. You'd kill me, I believe, if I tried that." Shipley told him that he was correct on that. "I thought so. And secondly, you'd also kill my momma if she were to call you spoiled if I was able to sleep with you. You'd probably kill me for that, too. Wouldn't you?"

"Yes. I don't like you, Scott. I have never liked you." He told her that he knew that, too. "Then why aren't you telling your mother that? You're a fucking grown man and should have stood up to her a long time ago."

"I don't know what to do about her." She asked him what he wanted to do. "Leave town. Just up and leave town and never look back. She's not nice to me at all. And when she is, I keep looking for the knife that she's going to be stabbing me with when I didn't do something that she thinks that I should have."

"Your life is your own. If I were you, I'd collect my shit and get out of there. I'm betting that you still live at home, don't you?" She started taping on the keys of her computer, looking for places that he could hide at should he leave his mother. "Do you have any money?"

He said that he didn't because his momma made him pay back what she had to pay for him to get out of jail the first time. Scott told her how he had community service that he had to do in order to have gotten out of jail. She could easily take care of that for him. As she was doing her search, she sort of half listened to Scott and his woes about his momma.

"You do know that you're a grown assed man, don't you? Stop calling her momma. Call her mother or mom, but stop…you're older than I am, Scott. Grow a set of balls and call her mom. Christ, she must have been so proud of the way she raised you." He cried. Just like a kid, he started crying about how she was being mean to him. "I'm going to kick your ass if you don't straighten up. What is the matter with you? Stop whining and listen to me."

She told him of the house that she had not too far from where her sister lived. Shipley thought about sending him to her sister's home, but Mandy would tear his ass apart if he started on that momma shit again. Not to mention crying like he was five instead of what his age really was.

"I want you to pack you some clothing. Not a lot. Only enough that you can carry in a duffle. Do you have one of those? Like from high school?"

Scott told her that he had two of them. "You don't need two. Just the one. Pack it full of your clothing and shit that you're going to need for the next week. Any money that you can lay your hands on, too."

"What about my momma...mom?" She told him that he needed to cut the strings before she did. "All right. See? I knew that you'd be mean to me if we were together. We're not even getting married — we're not, are we? — and you still treat me badly." She decided to ignore his question about them getting married.

"You're going to leave the house within the hour. Go to the library and stand there waiting for someone to come and get you. It will either be one of the Erickson men or my sister. Just keep your mouth shut and do what they tell you." He asked her if she was going to tell on him. "No, dumbass. You're going to be leaving home so that she doesn't know where you are. So I want you to get your shit together and be there in an hour. Do you understand me?"

"Yes, I'm packing my duffle now. There isn't much you can put in one of them, is there?" She told him that was the point. He was just going to leave. "All right. I'm going to walk to the library. I won't say anything to momma...mom because she's not home."

"Good. Go there, and I'm going to make some other phone calls. Just wait for one of them to come for you." He said that he would. Then he thanked her for her help. "You'll be able to thank me when you get out of town and never return. You don't need your mother any more than I did mine. Get your shit together is what you need to do."

Calling her sister, she said that she had company over and that she'd pick him up as soon as she could get the person to leave. It was Mrs. Landry. She told her what she was doing, and her sister laughed.

"I'll keep her here all night if that's what it takes to get him away from her. You just let me know what else I can do to help out." She said that she was going to call Dusty and see if he could help. "He just called here. I think he misses you. Anyway, he asked me if he could have dinner with me and the kids. I, of course, told him yes. So I know that he's not too busy right now."

After telling her sister thanks, she called

Dusty. After explaining what she was going to do, he was all for it. She told him, too, that her sister was entertaining Mrs. Landry, so that wouldn't be an issue.

"I'll give him some money too. I'm betting that he doesn't have anything on him." She told him that she was going to do that. "I will enjoy this. Just to get him out of our hair."

After hanging up with him, she called Scott back. He was at the library and was terrified that his mom was going to show up. Telling him where she was and that Dusty and Amanda were going to help him, he cried again. The damned man was driving her insane.

"Dusty is coming to you. Don't give him any shit, and get into the car. He knows where to take you. If you call your mom and tell her where you are, so help me, Scott I'll never help you again. In fact, I'll help your mother beat you up. Do you want this or not?" He didn't say anything for a few minutes. "Scott?"

"I see your Dusty. He's about here." When he was silent for a few moments again, she started to scream at him. "Thank you for doing this for me. I know that I need to get away, and you've no idea…I've tried before, but she pulls me back. I'm glad that I didn't marry you either. You're mean, as I've said, but I don't think that we would have made a good couple. You're just too bossy."

The line went dead, and she had to laugh. She supposed that was the only way that he could get the last word in was to simply hang up on her. Putting the phone back in the cradle, she waited to see if Dusty would get back with her. She was going to have to jump his bones soon or have to find her a battery-operated boyfriend. Spending her nights alone was for the birds when she had a perfectly healthy man who wanted her right where she could get to him.

Plowing through the rest of the paperwork, she was only interrupted once more when she'd gotten a call from Dusty telling her that he'd gotten Scott where he needed to be. That was good, she told him.

"He gave me his cell so he'd not call his mom when he realized that she was going to be pissed at him. Scott, like a lot of people, had no idea what her number was because it's been stored in his phone. I don't know that I'd know anyone's number if I was asked. I even put the one for your office in the phone so that I'd not have to remember it." She told him that she'd made it so that he could get through to her whenever he wanted. "I did wonder about that. All I had to do was to say my name and that I wanted your number and they connected me right away. Thanks for that. When are you coming home? I miss you."

"Friday." She looked at the calendar on the wall in front of her. "That's only a couple of more days. You can hang on until then, can't you?"

"I'm not sure. The house is a bigger mess than I thought it would be. August is asking me all kinds of questions about how we want things. Do we want tile? Carpet? I told him no on the carpet, so I hope that was all right." Shipley told him that it was perfect. "Good. I thought that you'd say that. Also, while I'm talking to you, what do you think about a pool? My brother has one and I think that Zander does as well."

"I'd love a pool. Also, a hot tub. I did notice that you didn't have one when I was wandering around." She decided to tell him the good news. "I have fifty-seven days until my retirement. I didn't realize that they would count my boot camp time in that. Yay for us. Also, I'm to see the president in a couple of hours. He wants to talk me into staying on. I'm so finished and want to be home all the time. Have babies with you and shit. I guess we should make plans to have sex, too. I mean, that is the best way to have kids, I've heard."

"Seriously? The best way?" Dusty laughed. "I would love that more than anything right now. I've been taking cold showers since you left."

"So have I." The two of them laughed. "I have to go. I need to get this shit finished so that I can go out instead of staying inside all the time. My time off was good for me getting around but now I'm stuck here with paperwork."

When she hung up with Dusty, she buried her head in the work to get it finished. She really did have a lot of it to finish up and was glad to see that the last file on her desk wasn't that complicated. Looking up, she was startled to see Vice President Hayden sitting across from her.

"You do know that you talk when you work, I guess." She said that she didn't speak in English. "No, I noticed that too. Latin, if I don't miss my bet. I'm to understand that you're going to be leaving us soon. Is that correct?"

"Yes." She didn't say anymore, but he

nodded with a sly smile. "I have an appointment with the president later this evening. Or am I meeting with you now?"

"Me. He's been called away. Something that I'd like for you to do but I know with you getting out, if you get your ass hurt now, there will be hell to pay. I'm to understand that you're marrying into the Erickson family?" She told him that she was. "They're a good family. At least the sons are. Their father was a bastard, but he's gone now. Martha Grable, she would call us on occasion to let us know how much she thought of them. Martha was my great-aunt. I'm glad that she had them around when she needed them. My uncle was a shit to her."

"I didn't know she had more than one son." He winked at her with a short laugh. "I don't know why you think that is funny, sir, but I don't understand."

"She didn't have another son, but that prick that...well, she was my godmother when I was born. And when I got older, I lived with her for a time. After that, I considered her my aunt. It's a bit more complicated than that, but you understand." She didn't but nodded anyway. He pushed a file at her that she'd not seen until then. "There is all the paperwork that you need to be free of the army right away. It's been signed off on and filed. The president and I wish you a happy life and one that is as much as you wish to make of it. I'm to understand that you have a house here as well. If you would allow the government to purchase it from you, we'll give you a good deal. That way, when you come for a visit, and I do hope that you will, you and your family will have someplace to stay that is not too inconvenient for you."

"I don't want to sound greedy, but I'm staying the extra time because of my benefits. Those are too good not to have, as you well know." He told her that she was getting them as well as a promotion that started the month before she left to rescue a little boy from a car accident. "Seth calls me too. Just to tell me how he's doing. He's living with his aunt with two other kids his age. He loves it."

"The young man wrote to us as well. Telling us how he'd been terrified, but you stayed with him even though you were hurt as well." She said it really wasn't that bad. "No, but it was enough to impress upon us how much you're willing to give back even when you're on vacation. How is your sister, by the way?"

"She's happier than I've ever seen her. The kids and her are having fun. Looking forward to being a family again around the holidays. I think that she's having fun, too, without her mother-in-law barging in to take the kids from her, too." He told her that he'd heard that. "I'm also thinking too that she's going to be dating again, too."

"Really?" He didn't look so much surprised as he did happy. She asked him if he was going to ask her out. "I'm forever looking for a beautiful woman to take my arm when I'm working. And I'd love to talk to her about a future together. I've been in love with Amanda since you introduced us when you were out of boot camp, and I was a senator."

"I didn't know that. I'm glad to hear that, too. But you'd better hurry and ask her out. There are a few men around that want to take her out too when she's ready." He asked her if she'd mind him dating her sister. "Not at all. I think that it would be good for the two of you. But you have to realize that her kids will forever come first in her life. If you've got a problem with that, then I suggest that you leave her alone."

"I would love to have her children in my life. I've been sort of beating around the bush to get information about them from you since I met her. Obviously, you never noticed, did you?" She thought about what he said and was surprised that she'd never caught on. "Good, that's the way that I love it. I'll call her tonight, then."

When he stood up, she did as well. He told her that he was going to miss her, and she pointed out that if he became a part of her family, he'd be sick of her in no time. He was still laughing when he left her there.

~*~

Taking Scott to the closest airport to put him on a flight out of the state was an eye-opener—at least the drive-in had been. The man didn't shut up about the things that his mother had made him do over his lifetime, starting with his first day of school. Things that while not heinous, they were things that weren't the sort of things that would get him in good with anyone he was around. Dusty thought that Scott's mother was one sick woman.

She taught him how to cheat on tests in the classroom—even in kindergarten. The sort of people to hang out with, which he told him had been anyone that wasn't a true American. Which to him was all wrong. Scott told him that no one was a true American anymore. That we'd all come from someplace else. He was taught how to steal things from the store was another thing that she'd taught her son from a very young age. Dusty was glad that the man was getting away from his mother. He might have been a first-rate person if not for her influence.

Giving him enough cash that he could buy a one way ticket, he told him to pick a place and go there but not to tell him his destination. He didn't want to mess it up for the other man by letting it slip where he'd gone. The man was nervous enough as it was.

Leaving him at the airport after getting him some things to use on the flight—a book, some snacks as well as a bag that he could carry on as he had literally nothing to take with him but a couple of shirts and some questionable underwear that had seen better days, Dusty was glad that the man was going through with this. It might take him a while to get his life on track, but this was a good first step for not just Scott but with those people who were around him all the time.

As soon as Dusty was out to his car, he looked at Scott's phone—having had it handed to him earlier, he saw that Scott had fifty-three missed calls and had twelve messages—all from his mother. There were text messages as well and after reading those, he was laughing as he found his way to the voicemails.

Each one that was there was from his mother. Christ, she got more and more angry as she went on and on. Twice, on the last few messages, she'd been cut off due to her rambling on about the things that she was going to do to him when he finally came back, and that seemed to piss her off more. The promises, because they were well beyond threats by the end, would have had the man running back home with his tail between his butt cheeks. He knew that it would him.

Pulling out his cell, he wanted to call Shipley to let her know what was going on now that Scott was out of their lives and working to get his own life on track. She was due home tonight, and he couldn't wait to talk to her. Just as he was going to call, she called him. He loved too that when it came up on his phone who it was, he had put "My

Wife."

"I have some wonderful news for us." She explained how she'd been given her retirement for her help in things both domestically and on foreign soil. There was also the added bonus perks she was going to get. Which, even though she nor Dusty needed the money right now, it was something that she'd worked very hard for and wanted to cash in on it. "I have insurance, too, as well as money for whatever kind of funeral that we have. For both of us."

"What about your house there? You mentioned that they might well want to purchase it." Shipley explained to him how that was going to work. "So that is a good perk. We can have a house there and here at home so that we won't have to share with strangers. I think I like that one best of all."

"Getting any of the perks that he gave us is something that I didn't expect. So I'm thrilled to death that I'm going to be able to cash in on something that I worked so hard for." They talked about the different aspects of living here or there and how much nicer it was going to be to not have to worry about anything from now on. Then she asked about Scott. "Just so you're aware, my sister said Alma has been asking around town as to where he might be. It was said that she thinks that one of you boys killed him off because he was competition in my hand in marriage. I'm hoping that by the time she gets around to asking us where he is, we have a plan."

"Oh, I have a plan. I don't have the slightest clue where he is. I took him to the airport, and he took it from there. Not that I have any intentions of telling her about the airport but I will be honest when I say that I don't know where he went. While there, I handed over the cash that I took with me so I could tell him to just buy a ticket, and that's what he did." She asked if he'd asked for advice. "Not at all on traveling. However, he did tell me things about his childhood that makes me feel sorry for him. Also, he told me that he thinks that she killed his father. But as he has no proof, he...he told me that he had no idea why he was pursuing you. Scott said that his mother had told him what to do and that he did it without question."

"Yeah, I'm beginning to understand where he was coming from more and more." They talked a bit more about Scott and the way that he'd been brought up, and with Shipley adding her thoughts, it's a small wonder that the man had ever been able to hold down a job, much less try and find someone to love him. "I'm happy for him. I'm glad too that you were able to make sure he understood that if he returned, you weren't going to be so helpful to him again."

"I really believe that he understood that more than he did me. He'll not return. And if he does, it will only be on the death of his mother. Even then, I'm not so sure. Scott was giddy if you can believe it. Thrilled beyond words that he was getting this chance when he really didn't feel like he earned it."

He pulled into the driveway of their home and sat out in his car, talking to Shipley. He had to laugh when she asked him if he was going to continue to call her Shipley or use her first name. At her laughter, he was able to tell her that he didn't care what he called her so long as she loved him. That, she told him, was a perfect line.

"I have to get going if I'm coming home tonight." He said he'd wait up for her. "I wish now I would have told you to drop me off. Now I'm going to have to drive home to see you. Not to mention, we still need to have a few times getting down and nasty with each other. I want you in so many ways that I can't think when I see you out in the yard with your shirt off."

"You tell me that when you're hours away? That's so unfair." Teasing her a little, he told her how he'd been taking the coldest showers, and if she didn't take him to her bed, then he was going to break something on his poor, abused body. "A man can only stay hard for so long before he begins to not have any kind of brain cells left. You do understand that, don't you?"

"I'm taking cold showers, too, just so you're aware. I've never been one to use sex toys, but with things the way they are now, I really think I might have to purchase us one. It seems like forever since I've had sex." He asked her if she knew what she was doing to him. "I do. I have been in all the shops here in town today to see if I could find something enticing that I could lure you to bed with. So far, I'm not having a great deal of luck, sadly."

"Honey, you could show up in just your panties, and that would be more than enough for me. Nothing at all would be even better." She laughed, but it was a sexy one. Breathless like and so full of promise. He smiled cunningly. "You keep this conversation up, and I'm going to meet you at the door hard and naked. What will my family think if I just stand around all evening with a hard-on."

"They'll wonder what took you so long in figuring out what to do with it." They talked like that for the next twenty minutes of so. At least long enough for her to get into the shuttle that was taking her to the airport to come home in. While waiting for her, he decided that there were things that he wanted to do to the house before she came home.

It wasn't too late when he remembered to order her flowers. Someone would meet her at the airport with them, and she'd know just how much he loved her. Also, the rose petals that he sprinkled all over the bed were next. He had made up a cheese and meat tray so that they'd have something to munch on between bouts of lovemaking as well. Going to the wine cellar, which he thought all of his family had one in their homes, he pulled out the best white that he had. Making a mental note to himself, he was going to invest in some champagne so that they'd have it round for special occasions like today.

It was what caused him to pause a moment at the top of the stairs. All moments with Shipley were special, he realized just then. He also had other thoughts filtering through his mind. When she had their first child, a boy or girl. Christmases spent with each other and children when they came along would be the best. They should have had some special occasions when they moved into this house together, he realized then. He was able to have some special times because of her retirement, but he wanted to make special days that didn't have anything to do with special occasions.

Just plain old Mondays would be a day to celebrate. A Friday as well. Smiling as he carted things up to the second floor, thankful that this part of the house was finished up, he enjoyed shaving for her so as not to give her beard burns when she came to him.

Just as he was running out of things to prepare for her coming home, he realized that she would be landing soon. Once she disembarked and was on her way home, it would be another hour for them to get together. After thinking about how much fun he was going to have tonight, and hopefully her as well, Dusty was dancing a jig around his living room when the front doorbell rang. Like they were laying on the button to get his undivided attention.

Looking in the little camera he was dismayed to find Alma there. The crazy woman had her cane pressing the button while she leaned into it. Almost as if she were going to come through the door and right into his lap. Opening the door, not caring at all if she fell on her ass, he jerked the door open.

Barely catching himself when she came into the room head over ass, he waited until she weltered her way up off the floor and stood up. He didn't dare get close enough to help her. He might be in a very forgiving mood, but he wasn't stupid either. Dusty asked her what the hell she wanted, as he was too busy to mess with her tonight.

"Where is my son?" He just stared at her. "Are you stupid like that woman is that my son is going to marry? I asked you a question. Where is Scott?"

"Now, why the hell would you think that I should know. I barely know you, and that's too much for one person to put up with." She seemed confused, and he didn't elaborate. "Well? When are you leaving?"

"I asked you a question. And I'm going to stand right here until you answer me. I know that you took him. One of you did, anyway. He's not answering his phone, nor is he coming home when I leave him a message." Still, Dusty stood there, not saying a single word to her. When she raised her cane up, he took an aggressive step in her direction. She lowered it slowly then. "Where is Scott?"

"I haven't any idea where he is. I didn't know that anyone would care about a nearly thirty-five-year-old man. He's single, so perhaps he's out looking to get laid." She lifted the cane about halfway up but didn't put it down again. "I'm a grown man, too, and if you think I'm going to allow you to hit me with that cane and not retaliate, then you're a bigger fool than I thought you were."

"I want my son. I'm not going to ask you again." He told her that repeating herself was sort of trying anyway. "Damn you, boy. Tell me where he is."

"I don't know." He pulled out his cell phone and dialed the police. "You can leave now, and I won't have to have you arrested, or you can hang around here, and when my wife gets home, she can shoot you for trespassing. Again. Now leave—" The police answered, and he told them what he had going on.

"We're out and about that way anyway, Dusty. We'll swing by and help you remove the woman. You say she just barged in?" He didn't but thought it was funny that they understood the problem. "We'll just have to run her in again if she's there when we get there."

She was still standing in his living room when the police showed up. After telling her to leave his home, Alma told the police that he'd kidnapped her son. The men around started laughing and snickering when she asked what they were going to do about it.

"Nothing. He's a grown man." The third time that had been said to her today. "I doubt very much that anyone has him locked up in their home, Mrs. Landry. You go on home, and the rest of us will pray that he's finally gotten some balls of his own and that he's lit out of here and never returns."

She left after Shipley showed up. Not

willingly, but she was gone all the same. It might have been because Shipley pulled her gun out and said that she'd help the police remove her from their home, but he wasn't sure. He didn't know but was thrilled to be able to lock the door behind that nasty old woman and be with his pretty new wife.

Chapter 5

It was nearly midnight when they finally made it up to bed. After having to file charges against Alma, they had to cool down. Mostly, it was her having to cool off after dealing with the woman. She'd never been as pissed off at someone as she was that woman. Alma accused them all of kidnapping her son and making it so that he didn't come home anymore.

"I hope he has left you." Alma drew back her hand and told Shipley that she was going to make her regret her words. "You do that, and you'll be pulling back a stump old woman. I'm not in the mood to fuck with you tonight. I've been making plans to have sex with Dusty, and you've been a fucking pain in my ass since."

"The things that come out of your mouth. What a disgrace to the America that I love." Rolling her eyes at the older woman, she wasn't the least bit surprised that she took offense to that as well. She was about the dumbest mother fucker that she'd ever encountered. "You'll tell him to come home to me this moment or I'll have to make you see reason. I will, too. He's my son. And so you know, I wouldn't allow him to marry you now if he begged me. You're not at all what I thought you'd be in a daughter-in-law."

"Good for you." After the police got over their laughing at the elderly Landry, they took her to jail. Trespassing was all they could hold her on for now but she was sure that she would be able to think of other things to charge against her if it came down to it. "Don't come back here, or I will shoot you, Alma. I've had enough of your shit."

After she'd left, she and Dusty sat on the deck out back and thought about anything other than Alma. They talked a bit about the pool that would be going in, as well as the hot tub that had been delivered just this morning. It wasn't full as yet but it would be before tomorrow night. There had been other deliveries that had arrived while she'd been gone, and she was thrilled to see that they'd all been set up or were in the process of them being put together. The two of them walked hand in hand to the bedroom and she smiled at the romantic way that Dusty had done their room.

The candles were being lit as she watched him. The trays of food, both of them having a different food on them, was a nice touch, and she found herself not a huge fan of chocolate enjoying the little morsels that he'd put on one of them. The meat and cheese platter had cut-out hearts of cheese. There were even hearts cut into the meat that looked so cute that she ate a couple of them while wandering around the room.

"I wanted things to be special." She nodded, unable to speak beyond the lump in her throat that had formed there. "I have wine, too. I wasn't sure if you like champagne, but I'm going to make sure we have some around for all the special occasions."

"I love it. And you." She picked up a couple of the rose petals and crushed them between her fingers. The scent, strong and heady had her smiling again at Dusty. "You've gone to a lot of trouble. And while I know that we were going to end up here tonight anyway, I love that you made an effort for it to be lovely. I guess I never thought of myself as a romantic, but I do love all this."

When he finished lighting the different candles, she joined him at the window. She'd noticed that the walls weren't painted as yet, but she didn't care. The room was theirs and she was going to be staying here for as long as she had with Dusty.

"All I've thought about all day is that I want to strip you down and make love to you. Taking each button through the holes that would reveal a little part of you to me. Touching you as well. Touching a part of you that I love, even though I belong to you, I want to mark you as mine forever and a day." The warmth had her shivering a little. The heat of his words was already marking her as his, too. "Do you have any idea how much I love you? How much you mean to me? All the words in the world couldn't come close to me being able to tell you how much I love you."

"Oh, Dusty. I can't believe how much I love you as well. It's like from the moment that we met, it's been leading up to this for us. Us. Doesn't that sound about as wonderful of a word as you've ever heard? It is everything to me." She pulled him down to her mouth and kissed him, letting him know without words that she wanted him as well.

When they parted, just their mouths, he picked her up in his arms and took her to the bed before setting her down again.

He was true to his word on preparing her for himself. The way that he unbuttoned her uniform shirt had her body anticipating his every touch. Her nipples hardened when he brushed his hand over her bra. Nothing about her uniform nor her underclothing was sexy, but he made her feel like she was. Even his breath over her mouth and throat had her sighing heavily.

When her bra was unhooked, she let out a long breath. Just as he was pulling it down from her shoulders and then over her breasts, he kissed her nipple and then suckled hard on just the very tip. Tangling her fingers into his hair had her pulling him closer to her, allowing him to take as much as he needed from her.

"I'm going to love making love to you, darling." She nodded her body seemed to be on high alert with him touching her. As if every cell in her body was alive just because of him. When he helped her to the edge of the bed, pulling her pants off as he knelt before her, Shipley had a moment of unease when she realized that he was going to feast on her. Something that she'd never enjoyed during sex. But she shouldn't have worried. Everything with this man was going to be new and exciting.

Lying her back on the bed, he pulled her bare legs apart and inhaled deeply. That small action alone had her breath catching, and her pussy soak. When his fingers slid up and under her serviceable underwear and removed them, she decided right then that she was going to make sure that she had sexy underthings for making love to Dusty for the rest of her life. He deserved so much more than some white grannie panties.

"You smell so good to me. Like your body is calling me home." He flicked his finger over her clit, and she cried out. Not with pain, though there was a bit of that from needing to come so badly. But he didn't give her much of a chance to move away from his seeking fingers when they were sliding in and out of her while he watched her face.

Each time he slid his fingers or his tongue inside of her, she could feel herself getting closer and closer to coming apart. If not for him holding her in position, she would have flown away by now, her body screaming for more from him.

"Come for me, love." She didn't need to be

commanded twice for that but bowed up from the bed, her head bent nearly to her forehead and screamed out her release. It was more than she would have hoped for. More than anything that she'd ever felt before either. Her body now belonged to him. Whatever he did to her now, she was going to cherish it as much as she did him.

After coming at his demand, she was up and down with each new sensation. He would beg her for her cum, tell her to wrap her legs around his head she'd do it. With each stroke of his fingers, she came apart more. It wasn't until he lifted his head that she realized that she was covered in sweat and far from satisfied with her multitude of releases.

Moving her around so that she was in the center of the bed, Shipley touched Dusty everywhere she could reach. His nipples, his navel. She kissed his throat and his shoulder, digging her fingers into him so that she'd not come apart. Just as he was over her, his body hard and his groin straining at his root, Shipley wrapped her hand around his shaft and felt it fill with hot, fresh cream. It had her coming again and again.

His slide into her was more than she could

have hoped for from a man. Shipley knew that he was thicker than any other man that she'd been with before, and he filled her well. As he started to move, his hands all over her body, she arched up against him again and again with each of his downward strokes. It didn't take her long before she was hanging on again when he touched the spot in her that ripped her ways of feeling about sex right out of her body. Christ, he was everything and more than she could have hoped for.

The climax started in the back of her throat and seemed to curl up from her toes to the top of her head. When she came, screaming out her release by calling his name, it was all she could do not to faint from the feelings. Finally, when she could hold on no longer, she slipped into an abyss that took her over the edge while she was still reeling from his moves.

~*~

Dusty held Shipley to him while he tried to get his racing heart to slow down. It was difficult, more than he thought that it should have been to get his heart to slow and his vision back. Rolling to his side, he pulled Shipley with him and was glad that she was out for now. He was clumsy in the big bed, and he wanted her to think that he was manly after having his head twisted off and put back on his body after a roaring climax like he'd just had. His body, protesting his pulling from her body, seemed to settle down when he was just lying still and not thinking about what the two of them had done. To him, it was one for the books. That was as true of a statement as he'd ever had, too. Closing his eyes, he knew that he'd sleep well tonight.

Dusty didn't know what time it was when he was heading to the bathroom when he realized that he was trembling. He didn't know what was going on until he had to grab onto the sink when he was standing at the commode. Christ, he was drained. More so than he thought he'd ever been in his life. Even his feet were tingling right now.

On his way back to the bed, he noticed that Shipley was getting up. Kissing her on her mouth, he grinned when she glared at him. He also noticed that she seemed to be just as much a lightweight as he'd been when he'd gotten up. It was all he could do to get back in bed with the cheese tray before she caught him wincing.

"I'm starving." She took a piece of ham from the tray and walked to get the bottle of wine and the two glasses he'd put up here. The chocolate and fruit tray was in her other hand, and he marveled at her being able to carry so much in one hand. He also noticed that she was bleeding at her wounds and decided that he'd have his brother look at them later. Dusty wouldn't have been able to live down his brother seeing him in such a state after sex. "How much wine did you want? I don't usually drink it, being on duty all the time, but this is special. Christ, you're good."

Laughing, Dusty fed her grapes and watermelon that was on the tray. He noticed that she didn't take the chocolate, having told him that she simply didn't care for the taste, and made himself a mental note. Not only was she not a diamond girl, but she wasn't a box of chocolates woman either. They settled on the bed, sharing food and talking about anything and everything that just popped into their heads.

He told her about his father and mother. And again, about how they had won the lottery so long ago. She told him about how she'd never played, having had so much fear of losing out on all the things that she'd worked so hard for. They talked about children as well.

"I don't know how many I'd like to have but I do know that twins run in our family heavily." He told her good, that he'd love to have little girls just like her. "Amanda and I are the first set of female twins born on my father's side of the family, and we're only the second set born into my mom's family. They were all surprised by her. My mom was super tiny, being able to carry twins. She and my dad parted ways about the time she found out that she was having us. He didn't want to ruin his body by having twins. I have no idea what sort of body that he had nor what he thought that her having us was going to affect him, but I don't think he was very kind about my mother's body either."

"Our mom left when Zander was just a little baby. I think that he might have been about two when she told us one night that she couldn't take us with her when she left and that we'd, as children, were supposed to figure things out for ourselves. I never thought about how selfish she'd been until recently. To leave six children in the care of a drunk and abuser wasn't even close to having a good relationship with us." She asked about Martha. "We did literally have our van break down in front of her house. Her son had hidden her can of money too high on the shelf for her to reach it to see if he'd left her anything. The house, the one that Locke lives in with Amy, was in poor shape, but it had good bones. We worked our tails off on the thing, too."

"It's a showcase now. Even when I would come home at times, I remember thinking about how the place had gone to shit. Amanda told me about some people that were helping Martha and I was happy. So long as you guys didn't take advantage of her. She was a nice elderly lady. I was sorry that she passed on."

"We were as well. Locke lived in the house after we all moved out. It was his idea that he go to college to become a nurse for Martha. At the time, she was getting around really well, but we all knew that it wasn't going to be long before she got to the point where she would need constant care." She told him that was the sweetest thing that she'd ever heard. "Locke was in love with her. I think that we all thought of her as our mom or, I guess, grandmother. Then, when Alex came along and moved into the house as Martha wanted, the two of them fell in love almost as quickly as you and I did. She also helped us out with our finances as well."

"What a romantic story." He kissed her on the nose. "I'm full now and sleepy. Are you going to get frisky with me again or can we just wait until in the morning? I have to say, I'm bushed right now. This was the perfect way to unwind."

"I'm glad that I could be of service." He gathered up the trays and bits and pieces that they'd gotten on the bed. Shipley stood up and gave the sheets a good shake that had him salivating again. The way that her breasts leapt with the sheet had him turned on again.

He was glad that she cuddled up with him for the first few minutes. Then, he had to back away from her when she started rolling around in the bed. She was a bed hog, he soon discovered, and was happy for the larger bed when she finally settled down. Smiling to himself, he wondered if she'd kick him out at any time and thought that he was going to be on his best behavior from now on if he wanted to be able to sleep with his new love.

Just before settling down to sleep, he thought of a couple of things that he needed to take care of in the morning. One of them was to take her to the courthouse to finally have their marriage official. Neither of them wanted a large wedding, so like his brother, they decided that they'd just do the courthouse thing and be done with it. He had asked his brother, Locke, to be his best man, and Mandy was standing up with her aunt. Amanda was going to do it, but she was worried for the baby Parker and so Mandy stepped into the void for her aunt.

By the time the sun was coming up, he had to get out of bed. He wasn't finished sleeping, his body protesting the fact that he was actually up, but he had other things to do and besides, Shipley had left him about an hour ago to go and talk to her sister.

While he didn't know what she had to talk to her about, he did concede that they were very close and probably were happy that they were settling down in the same country. He couldn't believe that the two of them were hard to tell apart. He knew which one was Shipley over her sister every time when asked. He picked up his office phone, his desk getting a once over before Shipley got home when it rang.

"I have three things that I need to clear up. Number one is that my insurance needs to be changed again. I'd rather leave it for Amanda; it's a goodly sum, but that doesn't feel right when you're going to be married to me." He told her to leave it the way it was. Amanda or one of the kids might need it someday. "All right. Thank you for that. The second thing is. And this would be totally up to you. How about we spend about a week in DC just having touristy fun? The house is still in my name for now, and I thought that we could go and see the sites. I've only been to DC a few times and never to do the malls and such. What do you think?"

"I think that's a brilliant idea. I've been a few times myself but I never got to go through most of the touristy things either. Not many of them anyway." She told him that she'd make plans for them to be picked up and driven around as it wasn't a place to own a car in. The parking, she told him was at a premium. "Maybe we can rent a couple of bikes to use as well."

"I don't know how to ride a bike." That surprised him, and when she told him that they'd not had the money for one when she'd been a child and that she didn't think that Amanda knew how to ride one either. "I had plans to learn, but the service was first in my life, and I didn't want to lose out on anything that was offered to me either."

"I understand. I'm surprised but understand. I can't...well, I suppose that you were right in saying that you didn't have the money for one. We didn't either and walked everywhere we went at home. Then, with us moving here, I found one in the old barn when we were cleaning up, and we all learned. I'll teach you."

"We'll see. I have lots of things that I want to keep my body in shape for, and riding and crashing a bike isn't on the list." They both laughed, and he couldn't believe how much he loved her. "All right. Mandy is waiting for us to get going. I'll see you at the courthouse in about twenty minutes. And so you're forwarned, I'm in my dress-up clothing as my sister and niece requested. I hope that's all right."

"It is. More than all right." He closed up his computer and was ready to head out the door when she told him not to forget to bring his cell phone. He'd forgotten it the other day, and she was still teasing him about it. However he had to come into his home again twice before he got to leave for the courthouse.

Once to get his cell phone, he couldn't believe that he'd forgotten it, and the second time was to change out of his jeans for a suit jacket. If she was going to be all formal, then so was he. And when he put on his suit and patriotic tie, he felt like he could take on the world and come out on top.

As soon as he was finally there, he felt about as ready as he'd ever felt. He was dressed up, he had gotten flowers for his one true love and they were going to be married in less than an hour. There wasn't anything that would have brought him down. This was, he knew that it would be his favorite day of all time. The day that he became a husband to the greatest woman in the world.

Chapter 6

"9-1-1, what's your emergency?" When no one said anything to her, Rogen repeated herself. "Hello, what's your emergency?"

"He's in the house." She found herself whispering back to the quiet voice on the phone, asking him his address. After giving it to her, the voice told her again that he was in the house. "He's looking for me, but I don't want him to find me."

"All right. What's your name?" He said that his name was Harlin Sharp. "All right, Harlin, who is it that is in your house, and why is he trying to find you?"

Rogen dispatched the police to the address and verified that the call was coming from the address that Harlin had given her. Waiting for him to speak again, she brought up the cameras that were in his area and tried to look at the house. All she could see was a black blob of some kind of car outside the home.

"He killed my mom a week ago. I've been trying my best to make sure that he can't come back but I think he's worried on account of the police not showing up." That was confusing to her, and she asked him what he meant. "Listen to me." His voice was sharp with her. "I said that the police didn't show up after he killed my mom, and that has him worried. About me telling on him. Are you paying attention to what I'm saying?"

"Yes. And I know that you're scared or nervous, so I'm going to let it slide about how you're speaking to me." She could almost hear him rolling his eyes when he answered her back with *whatever*. Putting him on mute, she told the police that the child, if he was one, was being too snarky to be extra careful. They told her to ask for details. "Where is your mother's body? Is it in the house with you?"

"Yes. Where else would it be? Are the police coming or not?" Not liking this at all, she told two more cruisers to go to the house. The kid was acting funny. And usually her instincts were correct on that. And most of the cops knew her well enough to know that she wasn't one to jerk them around, too. "Is. The. Police. Coming? Should I hang up and try someone else."

"Go ahead, and I'll cancel the police. Now, tell me where your mother's body is?" He said that she was in the basement and that since she started smelling the place up, he thought she'd be better down there. "Okay. Why didn't you call the police? Is it because you were afraid?"

"I'm not afraid of anything, you stupid bitch. Who are you?" Again, the sharp voice, almost like she'd hit a nerve with him. She told him her first name was Rogen. "Rogen? What sort of name is that? Can I speak to your supervisor?"

Alarm bells were going off in her head now. The kid was nearly screaming at her about her supervisor. Calling for one, she let him know what was going on and the issues that she was having with the caller.

"He's loud, for one thing. If there was someone in the house, he would have tipped them off by now. Also, he's not helping himself by threatening me that he's planning to hang up. I told him that I'd stop the police from coming, and that set him off again." Scott told her to turn on the mike again. "My supervisor is here. His name is Scott."

"She's a bitch." While not agreeing with the caller, Scott did laugh a little. "And are the police coming here? I've been waiting for them for what seems like forever. The alarm went off about an hour ago and there hasn't been anyone showing up of authority."

"The police are nearly there. Tell me why you think that this man is looking for you? You believe that, or he's said that?" The man sitting next to her took off his headset and stared at her for a moment before speaking to her.

"I know that address. There isn't a woman in the house that I've ever seen. Just an elderly man that is in a wheelchair." Rogen asked Scott how he knew that. "I'm boarding in the house across the street and I've been talking to the elderly man named Gross for the last few weeks. He said that his wife was dead and that he had no other children. He plays a good game of chess."

Relaying the information to the cops, she waited until they pulled onto the street before she told them to be careful again. Scott asked if he could see the house, just to make sure it was the same one when she nodded. It was, he told her and went back to work at his own cameras.

Scott hadn't been there for long before everyone was saying how he was all right. He didn't speak much. Made notes all the time about calls and the people around them. Never once had he said anything to her or the others but when asked, he was polite with his answers. Someone told her that he was coming from an abusive place and was truly afraid that someone was coming for him.

Rogen had heard it was his mom but didn't know if she believed that or not. He didn't strike her as a momma's boy, and figured maybe that was the point. He wasn't, and she wanted him to be. When the kid on the phone started getting louder again, she had contact with the officer first on the scene.

"He said that her body was in the basement, and he put her there when she started to smell the place up. It could be just as we were told, but one of the other dispatchers said that the house didn't have a female in it." Roger told her that he didn't think a woman was living there either, as there were no flowers in the front yard, and the trash can was filthy. "I'm not even going to ask you why you'd assume a woman would be planting flowers and cleaning trash cans."

"My mom. She keeps hers clean by rinsing it out after pick-up day. It's dead summer, and those suckers get really nasty. As for the flowers, every other house on the street has them planted. This house looks like it's not had any kind of touch to it in months to years." She didn't care for Roger's take on what was going on but she let him speak. For all she knew, there wasn't anyone planting his flowers. But it made her nervous for the police to be going into the house.

The police, as it turned out, were a bit more cautious than she could have hoped for. After going into the house from the front and back, they were greeted with gunfire that blasted into her headset like she was right there with them. It wasn't until the smoke, whatever that meant to them, was cleared before they were able to answer her questions about how they had faired.

"We'll need the wagon." She dispatched the coroner to the scene and then asked about the kid. "He's not a kid, Rog. I'd say from looking at him, he's between twenty-five and thirty years old. You were right in that this was something eerie going on. He was set up with enough shit to take out the city block. Also, he had a list of things that he was going to fulfill. After killing as many cops as he could, he was going to head to the grocery store on Eleventh to kill kids. You did right in warning us, honey."

Their town was small, so hearing someone call her by her nickname wasn't unusual. But it was frightening to know this person was out to kill a lot of people. Everyone knew everyone's business here. Even if you didn't have any business for them to get into, they weren't above making shit up about you. That was why she'd been so surprised that a man like Scott had moved here and set himself up in a boarding house. Like this was the spot where he was going to be living out the rest of his life.

"Are you all right?" She asked Scott what he meant when they both went on break at the same time. "That call? Did it rattle you? I think that it would have me. And I've not been doing this as long as you have."

"It did, thanks for asking. I think that since we rarely get any calls that involve the police, mostly it's missing cats or something, this one got on my last nerve. In a way that had me second-guessing myself." Nodding, he sat down beside her in the small cafeteria and smiled. "You're new around here."

"I am. I've lived here for about a month now. And this is my first job that I'm enjoying. I thought that I liked the job I had before coming here, but this is my own, and I love it." She didn't understand that but didn't comment. "You're not at all like anyone else that lives around here. You seem, I don't know, more resigned to the fact that you live here. Is it that bad?"

"No, not really. I used to live in a bigger city but I kept losing myself there and decided to come home for a change. My sister and her husband live not far from this building, and I can hang out with them when I'm off." They spoke about the town and the residents that were there. "I was thinking earlier about how I've not heard a great deal about you. You must be keeping to yourself pretty well."

He stood up and sat down when Roger came into the room with them. He'd come by to check on her like she was some sort of delicate rose or something, and it seemed to spook Scott a bit. After telling them what had gone down at the house, Mr. Sharp being killed, and the elderly man that had lived there was dead as well. He didn't know for sure, Roger told her but he thought that the elderly man was gone long before tonight and that the suspect had taken advantage of the situation.

After he left, Rogen looked at Scott. "You're on the run, aren't you? Or you're some kind of weirdo that I need to avoid. Listen up, buddy, I don't take kindly to a stranger marking me as some kind of trip that they want to play with." He laughed.

Rogen didn't know why but she thought that it had surprised the man as much as it had her. He also looked rusty at having a sense of humor. Leaning back in her chair, she asked him point blank what he was doing there.

"I want to tell you. However, I'd hate for that to make it so that you don't want to see me or talk to me again. I like you." She snorted, and he laughed again. "I've run away from home and my mother to start my life over here. I was helped by some really nice people to not only leave my mother behind but to also go someplace where no one cares where I'm from or what I do so long as it doesn't bother them. I think I got that by coming here."

"You're serious." He nodded and told her how he'd been given money for a ticket and decided that he didn't want to go far. Not because he wanted to return home but so that his mother would think that he had, and staying close seemed a better idea. She stared at him for a full two minutes. "Why? I mean, why did these nice people help you? Not that it's really any of my business, but I was just wondering."

"I ask myself that very question everyday since. It's not like I was nice to them. I was a pest, as a matter of fact. And was set to marry a woman I didn't love or wanted in my life simply because my mother told me to do it. She thought that she'd be a good person to have around since she was a doctor and had strong arms. I kid you not. I thought it was as good a reason to marry as any, I suppose, and became a pain in the ass to this other woman and her soon-to-be husband. For all I know, they're probably married by now." When she asked him where he was from, she immediately told him that she didn't want to know. "Thank you for that. I would tell you if you asked but I'm a little shy around all that many people knowing where I'm from. I'm...well, I'm terrified that my mother will find me and drag me back to her level. I'm enjoying being my own boss—that was another thing that I did all wrong. I was a terrible employer to those that answered to me. Now I can see that I wasn't even as nice as I thought I might well have been. I was just a pain in the ass all the way around."

"Do you feel like you've changed all that much?" He nodded telling her that he was living in the boarding home that Ms. Archer owned and he was enjoying all the other people that came and went. "Ms. Archer was my teacher in grade school. Even back then, I thought her odd and old."

She talked to him during their lunch hour. Also, when they got back to their stations between calls. Scott Landry, she remembered his name now, was a nice person. While she didn't know him before coming here, she would bet too that he had to work extra hard on breaking some of the habits that he used to have. Like him calling his mom his momma was a biggy to him. A habit that he was trying hard to break.

After work, they walked to her sister's

house. She wasn't staying there but would watch their kids for an hour or so nightly. It helped Lily get dinner on the table and Mark when he got home to unwind without the kids wanting him to play with them when he only just walked in the door.

She didn't do it every night, she loved her nieces and nephew but they were even a bit much for her at times. Not wanting to think about their nights when she didn't come over, Rogen was glad to be able to help them out. Besides, she got herself a good home-cooked meal out of it.

Lily invited them to stay for dinner which was fine by her. They just accepted Scott like he'd been around forever, and it felt like it. By the time she was ready to get herself home, not far from her sister's home, she thought that the two of them were friends. Not good ones, but friends all the same. It made her feel good when he told her that he trusted her with the information as to where he'd come from. It really wasn't far, only about fifty miles from where they were right now.

Scott didn't pressure her into anything on their way back to her house. He did take her hand into his when there were people coming toward them. She liked that. While she had no intentions of falling in love with the man, she found herself looking forward to tomorrow so that they could get to know one another more. Rogen didn't know if that was nutty or not and figured she'd not look too deeply into things right now.

~*~

There was a great deal of speculation going around as to where Scott had gone. She supposed that she could have looked for him but didn't want to mess with him anymore. Shipley decided that he might well have been a different person than he ended up being if not for his mother. Christ, she was a nightmare.

Alma was now in jail. She was going to be there until her court hearing was taken care of next week. Having little to no money kept her in jail without anyone paying her bond, and Shipley thought that it was funny that she actually was still going on about how she was going to be her daughter-in-law soon, and the least that she could do was to bail her out. Not only had she told her no, but she told her hell no she wasn't going to do that. Then there were the things that she was spreading around about them kidnapping her son and forcing him into hard labor. Like they had a camp someplace that had him in chains and balls working on the railroad line or something. Idiot.

Today was her first full day without having a job to go to. Even when she was on her little vacation to help out her sister, she knew on some level that she was going to have to go to work eventually. But this, staying home because she could, was boring as fuck.

She needed something to do. Not a job that she was going to go to daily but something that made it so that she had something to look forward to a couple of days a week. It wasn't as if she needed the money; Dusty had put her name on all the accounts that he had and she was a very wealthy woman. It was heady to know that she could spend as much as she wanted and not worry about it. She didn't, of course. That would be just stupid. She was picking up her phone when it rang, and she wasn't surprised to see that it was Dusty. He started the conversation out by telling her how much he loved her.

"That's the perfect way to start out a conversation. What's up?" He told her that he was going to go to the school after he got his work finished up and would like for her to meet him there. "What's going on?"

"They're needing their field redone. While I will say that it's in need of a good workover, I'm not sure as a family that we should be responsible for the entire thing. I'd like for you to have some input on it." She told him what she thought. "That's brilliant. If they don't raise enough with us matching it, we'll just not have to worry about it. Thanks. I knew that you were a good idea person."

"Matching them dollar for dollar is how the schools where we went were able to raise enough money for the football field when I was going to college. Not only did they exceed in the amount, there was enough money to have the bleachers redone as well. Also, they dedicated the field to all the fallen soldiers that had lost their lives during wartime." He told her again that she was brilliant. "Not so much. Just know that if you pay for whatever they want, they'll be hounding you to death for everything. This way, if they don't raise enough to make it work, then it's all on them."

"How about you meet me in town for lunch? I have one more meeting today with the board of directors at the hospital. Also, the police. They want to make sure that Scott hasn't been killed or something equally nefarious. I told them what happened, but they want it on record. I'm not so sure about that part. It might come back to bite me in the ass. Or worse yet, his mother to get wind of what happened. I honestly don't have any idea where he went, and that's all I'm going to say to them." She told him that she'd love to meet him for lunch and that she was leaving the house now to pick up the things that they'd ordered. "Oh, I forgot about that. The post office has several boxes there that they'd rather we pick up. Bring my truck."

After getting off the phone with him, she decided that it was as good a time as ever to go and see Alma. She'd been calling there nonstop for the past several days, and she wanted her to stop. It had been a month since she was ordered by the courts to stay away from her. Shipley didn't understand why calling all the time wasn't included in that. As soon as she was in the station house, she knew that something had happened.

"What is it?" She was ushered into an office and then asked to have a seat. "I don't want to sit down. I want information. Either give it to me, or I'll find it. Either way, I'm going to have the information."

"She's gone. I mean, she's dead. She died." She rolled her eyes at the officer and asked him what had happened. "I don't know, honestly. I mean, she might well have died in her sleep. But it's...she's going to the medical examiner's office now. I mean, they have to pick her up. Not pick her up like physically but—" She slapped him. Hard too.

"Now. Take a breath and tell me. I got that she's dead and that the medical examiner is coming to get her. When did you find her?" He told her right after breakfast. "I take it that she didn't eat then."

"No. That's what alerted us. She didn't bitch about her meal." He looked at her hard. "You hit me."

"Yes, and I'll do it again if you fucking don't get to the story. So she didn't bitch about her meal, and you decided to check on her. What did you find?" He nodded as if he was understanding that she was going to hit him again if he didn't answer her questions. "Donald. What the fuck is wrong with you?"

"I've never seen a dead person before." She told him that they don't tend to hurt the living. "You think not? I have a feeling that she's going to be haunting these cells for a good long time. All she did was complain about everything that we did for her."

"Focus." He nodded again. "Let me give you a word or two of advice. Don't talk to families that have lost a loved one. You really suck at it. So she's dead, and you don't know much more than that."

"She left a note. I think that has me freaked out, too. Like she knew that she was going to— please don't hit me again. I'm better now. But she left a note about her son." He looked at her hard. "You didn't kill him off, did you? I mean, I'd not blame you for all the crap that he pulled on you, but you didn't, did you?"

"No. I sent him on a trip away from his mother so he could get his life together." He nodded and told her that was what Dusty had said. "Then why are you asking me about him? Christ, it's a wonder that anyone around here uses you guys. You all must have a common brain cell that you share. What else happened that has you so freaked the fuck out? Is it the note? Who did she write it to?"

"You. She…want to read it? I did. I didn't think that you were the one she was talking about until I told my boss what had happened. He said that you were supposed to marry her son or some bullshit like that." She said she was never going to marry him. "No, I know that, too. You married Dusty. Congratulations on that, by the way."

"Thank you. Can I have the letter?" He said that it was in evidence and that the police, other than him, were holding onto it for now. "Then tell me what it said so that I can deny whatever she had to say about me."

"Just what I said. That you were an ungrateful person for not bailing her out with you being her future daughter-in-law and all. I don't know that she ever really believed that part. I don't think that she had a very high opinion of either you or Scott. Is he still alive?" She told him again that he was, but she didn't know where he was. "You said that. I'm just testing you now. I'm not as nervous anymore. But I'm betting that you've not seen a dead person either, have you?"

"I have. Probably more than you and every

member of this force will see in their lifetimes. Now, who is the M.E.?" He had to explain what the medical examiner was. "What do you mean you don't have one. You just told me that someone was coming to pick her up."

Donald started nodding but told her that the office was picking her up. But they didn't have one here that they could use. They had to wait for someone from another county could get around to doing the…he called it work up on her. The man wasn't going to last that long if he kept talking like he was. Donald might have been better suited to a job in a grocery store. Then she mentally told herself that he'd not be good at that. Too much blood and dead things around.

"You can do it." She asked him what he was talking about. "The work on her. I don't remember what—autopsy. You can do that, can't you? I mean, I could ask the hospital if it's all right with them, but you could do it, right?"

"I can't do it, not if she is blaming me for her death." He said that he'd never thought of that. "I could assist if you can find a doctor willing to do it. But as far as me being alone with the body, that's not going to work for a great many people."

"I'm going to call the hospital now. That's where they usually take the bodies. Let me see what I can find out." She sat down in the chair and waited for the man to return. She was going to suggest to whoever was in charge that Donald be given a desk job. The man didn't know what he was doing and it was going to cost the station a lot of grief if someone didn't sue them first. While she waited, she called Dusty.

After telling him what she'd been told, as well as her opinion of Donald, he said that he was sorry. Telling her to call Locke. He might know someone in that field who could assist in the autopsy. If not, then she'd have to wait on the results.

"I don't know what she might have died from, but I'm betting it was her heart. She had to be at least a hundred or so pounds overweight. I remember Scott telling me that the doctor was forever putting her on a diet, but she didn't follow it. But I won't know until someone confirms it." He asked her if she'd done that sort of work before. "Yes. There were so many men and women who would die, and someone had to take charge of the outgoing work. There would have been bodies lining the walls if we didn't have people there to do the work."

"I can imagine." He asked her to hold on. That his brother was there. He didn't say which brother, but she would bet that any and all of them would help out if they were asked. "All right. Locke is making a phone call. He told me that he'd get back to you in a few minutes. In the meantime, I'm going to be finishing up here with the campaign that I'm working on to raise the funds for the school. Thanks for that."

When the phone beside her rang, she didn't answer it. It wasn't her phone, and it could have been someone having an emergency. It was about two minutes after the phone stopped ringing that Donald returned to tell her that the call was for her. She picked it up on the first ring.

"Sergeant Shipley." The person on the other end of the call laughed. "If you called me for a chuckle, then you're going to be sadly disappointed. I'm busy here."

"It's David Hathaway." It took her a few seconds to know who that was. "Locke called me and asked me if I could make it so that you're the county medical examiner. I whole heartily agree

with him on you being the best man for the job.
I'm sending through—"

"Hold on there, Buster. I didn't say I wanted
the job. And in the event no one told you, Alma
blamed me for her death." He said that he trusted
her to be fair. "Well, I don't know that I want the
job."

"Did you know that that county alone is
backed up in examines by forty percent? The work
they need done needs to be done by someone who
can be trusted. And since I trust you more than
most doctors I know, I'm going to make sure that
the county knows to piss you off is to piss me off.
Do this for them, and I'll owe you a big favor. I
don't say that to many people, so you know." She
told him that she just got out of working for him.
"Yes, you did. And I'm glad to have done it. But
you might want to remember that you're a small
county, and there are fewer than ten unexplained
deaths a year there. Not a lot to keep you out of
your new home if you were to take the job."

"I don't want...don't I have to be voted in or
something? I mean, that's the way it works around
here, doesn't it?" he laughed and asked her if she
was looking for someone to vote her in or was

she discrediting his being able to tell her she had the job. "Both, I guess. I'll do it, but I'm sure that people are going to bitch."

"Doubtful. With you doing the work, that means that people will have their death certificates to be able to open accounts that might otherwise be closed to them. I'm thinking that, too. If you never say anything to anyone, no one will ever know." She told him she liked that idea. "I do as well. So can I count on you to work for me again?"

"No. But I'll work for the county, and that's all I'm going to say about it." She made her way to the hospital and asked where she was to be stationed. The board was there, too, welcoming her to the job and telling her what an asset she was going to be. She'd see, she thought to herself, if she was going to be an asset or not.

Chapter 7

Locke was assisting her with the backlog of bodies that were in the county. There were only seven, but she was pissed off because there were seven of them that hadn't been done. By the time she was ready to leave for the day, she and Locke had gotten nearly all the bodies identified, and most importantly, the office of the county medical examiner cleaned up enough so that they could use the office. It had been emptied out for nearly ten years, she told him.

"While there were no rats in the place, there were enough stink bugs in the room that would have qualified for a colony." He laughed. "I kid you not, Dusty. It looked like there were thousands of them in every corner of the room. Locke and I will never be able to look at a bug again without being sickened by them. Gross. And I've been overseas and thought that I'd seen it all."

"I'm glad that you were able to help out. I know that no one is to know, but I was stopped on the street twice today on the way home in having people ask me if you'd gotten to their relative as yet. I guess Mr. Jones died over a month ago, and his family had been at a standstill in getting things done in all that time. I was also told that the government gives veterans a marker when they pass as well."

"They do. Though I thankfully haven't had to look into that as yet. Tomorrow, we're going to get started. I'm so glad that Locke is going to be with me. He said that he has to work a little bit in the office, and this will be perfect for his degree. I didn't know he wasn't a doctor, to be honest with you. I had no idea that he was, as he calls himself, a plain nurse. He's far from plain anything if you ask me." Dusty told her that he'd gotten the degree to help out Martha, the woman who had helped them in so many ways. "That's what he told me, too. That she'd been better to you guys than your mother had ever been."

"More than anyone could have asked for." She asked him about dinner. They were supposed to have dinner with Demitrius tomorrow night as he was trying new foods out. "When I saw him at noon, he was picking up things from the grocery store. He said that he was going to have a salad, too, which he was really hoping went over well. I don't know what he meant by that, but I'm willing to try things."

"It's going to be one of those foo-foo salads, I'm betting. I can't stand those kind of things. I want salad stuff, not fruit. If I wanted a fruity salad, then I would get one. But only tomatoes and lettuce belong in a salad. Cucumbers, too, but nothing else. That kind of thing is supposed to be a side dish." Laughing, he asked her about onions. "Occasionally, you can have them in there so long as they're pickled. I love pickled onions."

"I'll have to take your word on that. I don't care for anything pickled." They spoke more about the dinner tonight and what they might be eating. Shipley wasn't the adventuresome type of person with her food. "That's probably because you've only had army messes. I'm betting you didn't get too many fresh burgers, did you?"

"Not where I was." They talked a bit more about food and the kind of things that Demetrius usually cooked for them. "I've never had lamb before. Unless you count having gyros. That's a good food, if you ask me. Also, I'm not a huge fan of pizza if there are other things on it besides meat and cheese. Regular meat, not chicken."

"Honey, I think that chicken is considered regular meat as well." She said it didn't belong on a pizza. "How do you feel about pineapple on a pizza then?"

"I'm hanging up on you. Those are fighting words." They were both laughing by the time she was home. Putting her phone away, she went into the house to be greeted by small arms and her favorite family. Parker wasn't too old, but she was learning that her aunt loved hugs, so that helped, too. She'd forgotten that they were babysitting the kids tonight as her sister had a date.

"How many dates have you had with Brad now? Do the Secret Service get in the way of you guys having a good time?" Amanda told her that they were just friends. "Sure you are. And I'm your uncle."

"Really? And all this time, I thought that we were identical twin girls." Amanda did look like she was happy with dating the vice president.

"Tonight is a huge deal in that I'm going to be present as his date to a lot of other dignitaries. With David having the flu, Brad and I have had to step in some for him. Have you heard if he's doing better or not?"

"I haven't, though I did hear from his secretary that he's supposed to be better in a couple of days. Admit it, you're having a blast." Amanda said that she was and that Brad was making her feel so special. "He'd better if he knows what's good for him."

The car showed up for Amanda about the time the pizza did. Brad paid for the pizzas for the kids and tipped the man an extra hundred for not saying who had paid. Of course, that went out the window as soon as he posed for a selfie with the man. Sometimes, she wondered where their heads were.

Parker was about eight months old now and was able to gum a crust really well. Mandy, of course, liked her pizza hot and spicy just like she did. People had been telling her for months that Mandy could be her clone, and of course, she took that to heart. She did have some special connection with the little girl.

After dinner, they headed to the living room for movie time. She couldn't believe how much fun they were all having, so when the front door buzzer sounded, she didn't want to go and answer it. Sending Dusty to answer the door, she was surprised when he yelled for her from the front hall and told her to come to him. She stood there staring at the man and woman for a little bit before she knew who it was.

"Christ, Scott. You look like a new man. And who is this lovely person with you?" He introduced them to Rogen and said that she was his new wife. They'd only been married for a couple of weeks. "You heard about your mom then?"

"The president called him." Rogen was a very beautiful woman, and Shipley could see that she loved Scott very much. "We worked together as dispatchers. It's been a whirlwind sort of ride for us both. We're also having a baby."

She didn't know who was more excited, Scott or Rogen, about having a child. When they joined them for movie night, it was all she could do not to tease Scott about his prior opinion about having children. Shipley thought that he looked like he'd invented having children and didn't care who knew it. They left about ten and she and Scott took the kids up to bed.

"Do you suppose that your sister will be getting married again?" She asked him if he meant Brad. "Yes. Do you know any other men that your sister has been dating?"

"No. I mean, I never thought of that. Do you suppose it's gone that far? I wasn't kidding her when I asked about the Secret Service around all the time. I do wonder how that's been working for the two of them. Also, Brad told me that he's been in love with Amanda since…well before Fred came along. And she looks so happy. Perhaps it will come down to her having a wedding again. I hope so. For both of them."

"I do as well. And he already loves the kids." She and Dusty talked about all the things that would be something of an issue with her marrying the VP. But none of them were insurmountable that they couldn't pull it off. "I don't know a lot about kids, but I've been keeping an eye on the kids when he's around. He never treats them in any way but as little people. Even Parker is a bit in love with him, too."

"She calls him Da-da." She just stared at

Dusty. "It was the last time Brad was here. He was holding her in his arms while Amanda was getting the kids off the bus, and I heard her. It shocked Brad, I think, but he never said anything to her. He didn't deny it, I mean. I think that he'd make a great dad. Why hasn't he married before now?"

"I never thought to ask him. Do you suppose he was waiting on Amanda to make a decision?" Dusty shrugged and told her that he hadn't any idea. "Me either. But I'll talk to my sister when she comes to get the kids tomorrow. I did tell you that they were staying all night. It's too far for Amanda to come back tonight." She cocked her head. "I just thought of something. If they do get married, that means she's going to be moving to DC and taking the kids with her."

"I should hope so." She growled at him. "What did you think was going to happen, love? That they'd carry on this relationship and make it work with the distance between them? No. If Brad doesn't ask her to marry him soon, I'm going to be very disappointed in him. He's more in love with her, if you can believe it than I think that any other couple I know is. Except for you and I. We carry all the love between us."

"You're insane." When they went to bed that night, she kept thinking about how it would work out between the two of them. She was just getting used to having her sister around all the time, and now she was going to leave her. What would happen if he were to run for the White House? Then she'd be out of that time, too.

She told herself that she was being selfish. Her sister deserved a life as much as she did, and her thinking about how it would affect her was simply mean. Getting up and leaving the bedroom, she wasn't the least bit surprised when her cell rang. It was her sister.

"What's happened? Do I need to come there and kick someone's ass? You know that I will." Amanda laughed and said that it was all good. "Then why are you bothering me at two in the morning?"

"Brad asked me to marry him." Shipley sat down hard on the stairs that she'd been standing on when her phone rang. "I've not told him yes yet. I wanted to talk to you first."

"Why?" She said because she was her sister. "No, I mean, why haven't you told him yes. And what on earth do you think I'd have to say about *you* getting married. Nothing at all. You're my sister, not my ward." Amanda started crying and that hurt her to her core.

"I just got you home with me and now I'm the one that will be running off. I don't know what to do. He had this beautiful ring for me. You should see it. It's the same stone as yours, but I love it so much more. And then there are the kids. What if they don't want me to get—"

"Hang on a minute. Just... Seriously Amanda, I don't think the two of you could be in any more love than you are right now, and then you have the rest of your lives to fall more in love." Amanda called her a romantic. "No, I'm a realist. You love each other so much. In fact, I think that the two of you have been in love since before you started dating. As for the kids, Amanda loves him. You know that if she had trouble with him, she'd tell you. And Parker is already calling him dad."

"When? When did she say that to him?" She told her that Dusty had seen it. "He never said a word about it. Oh, that helps so much. I don't know what to do about you. I can't lose you again. You're all the family that I have left." She pointed out that she had the entire Erickson family as well as her own kids.

"And you won't lose me. You do remember that we have a house in DC, don't you? And it's not that far away for us to just hop in a car and come see you. Right?" She told her that she could come and see her too. "Yes, but I don't know how feasible that will be with the Secret Service having to follow you around all the time. But we'll cross that when we come to it. And I don't know if you knew this or not, being that you just called me from there. I'm only a phone number away."

"There is that. But I'd want you here to help with the planning of our wedding. It'll have to be huge because of who he is and all." Shipley remembered that her sister hadn't had a large wedding, even though that was what she wanted at the time. "You'll be my matron of honor."

"No, I'm going to be giving you away. Mandy will be your maid of honor. Right there next to you, where she belongs. You know she's kind of stubborn, and that's where she's going to be anyway." They both laughed. "Parker and Fred will be there as well with one of the brothers. They'll love that they can be a part of their mother's big day."

After talking to her sister for another ten minutes, they decided that it was much too late for them to be making wedding plans and closed their connection. She knew that she'd sleep better and that Amanda would as well. Shipley was sad, sad that her sister had been so upset, but she was also feeling like she'd been sad too for no reason. So long as Amanda was happy then everything in her world was all right as well.

"Did you talk to her?" She smiled when Dusty spoke to her from the dark room. Telling him that it was all settled, he rolled over toward her and curled around her body. "I love you, Shipley. Do you regret not having a large wedding, too?"

"You knew that they were going to get married?" He said that Brad had asked him if it would be all right with her that he asked her sister. "He could have asked me, you know."

"And you would have turned him down. You needed to hear from Amanda, and once you did, it was all right. You know as well as I do that she's first in your life." She wasn't sure about that and told him so. "I know that she's your number one fan and the other way around. I'm all right with that, so long as I'm a very close second. I am, right?"

"Forever." She wanted to tease him but couldn't bring herself to do that. It was too late for that anyway. Snuggling up under his chin, she wrapped her arms around him and held him tightly. There was a lot to be said for having someone you love so close to you that it was like you were one person.

~*~

Dusty laid all the paperwork out in neat rows and was ready for his family to show up. This time, when they had their monthly meeting, he was going to be prepared. It had been a real eye-opener when he'd sat down at his desk and saw all the things that he'd been putting off in favor of spending time with Shipley. Grinning to himself, he thought of last night and the way that she'd met him at their bedroom door completely nude. Christ, the woman was so special to him.

He'd thought that she was asleep when he'd opened the door. Crying out a little when she said his name, Dusty thought for sure that she was sleepwalking. But putting out his hands to guide her to the bed made him have the biggest surprise of all. Her warm breast filled his hand, and he couldn't have moved if a gun had been pointed to his head.

"I have some news for you." He told her that he would have to wait until later, that he was busy examining her. "Oh, well, have you noticed anything different about my breasts, doctor sir? They feel much larger to me."

"I'll have to get a closer look." When she moaned as he took her breast into his mouth, he wanted to take her right then. But she'd been in a playful mood, and he wanted her to have her fun.

"Well?" He grinned again, telling her that he was going to have to let her know in a bit. That it took further investigation, and he was one very thorough man. "Good. Also, you should understand that they're tender, too. Just a little, so be nice to them. Their job duties have ramped up."

It took his addled mind a bit more to understand that she was serious. After having her ask him twice to be gentle, he pulled his head from her and looked at her. Dusty could see, too, that whatever had been going on then, she was happy about it. Then it hit him.

"You're pregnant?" She nodded. "You're going to have a baby. Is that why you're tender?

When?"

"Yes, I'm going to have a baby in about eight months." She pulled his hand down to her belly — still flat from all the exercising she'd been doing in the service. "Not just any baby either, I'm going to have *our* baby."

Dropping to his knees, unsure of himself for a moment, he laid his head on her belly and listened. His child was there, he had told himself. They had made a baby, and it was right there. Pulling Shipley closer, he tried to hear anything that would tell him that his child was growing there, but all he heard was her belly gurgle. Laughing, he looked up at her.

"I went to the doctor today. I thought about doing the test myself, but I was sure that if it came back positive, I'd think that I screwed it up or something. Then, when he called back with the news, I had to call him back twice to ask him if he was sure. I'm positive that he thinks that a loony is now working in the hospital and that he's going to have to keep an eye on me so that when I do have the little guy, I'll not lose him."

"Him? You know it's a boy?" She told him that she didn't know, actually but she was guessing.

"Twins? Do you suppose we'll have twins like you and Amanda? I'd be happy with anything we got but I'd so love to have twin girls. That look just like you."

He stood up and carried her to the bed. It was funny to him, even now, that he had taken so much care in lying her on the bed and covering her up. He also should have figured out that she wouldn't allow him to pamper her too much before she put her foot down. His little momma was going to be a wonderful mother.

They had made love slowly that night. He couldn't help but worry, too, about him poking at her. Of course, in his stupidity, he had said that to her that he didn't want to poke anything important, and she rolled out of the bed laughing. It had been an innocent comment, made in the heat of the moment and she laughed at him for hours — more than likely was still getting a giggle out of his comment even now.

"Dusty?" He looked at his brother, wondering why he was in their bedroom for a second. "You look goofy. What the hell is wrong with you? You're looking sappy, I was going to say, but that's not it. You and Locke are forever looking sappy now that you're married. What's up?"

He couldn't tell him. Dusty wanted to shout it to the world but he couldn't. Not until Shipley had her first appointment. She wanted to be positive about the baby when they told everyone, and she was still, him, too, wondering if they had messed up the lab work or something like that.

"Just being sappy. Can't a man be in love with his wife and get sappy over her? Shit, August, it's the best feeling in the world to be sappy about someone." He told him that he'd have to take his word for it. "You might feel this way soon enough. I know that I can't help but hope that the rest of you get someone to be sappy over as well. You'll love it."

"Nah. I'm not a man for being caught up with one woman all the time. I want to play the field. If I do meet someone special, she's going to have to be all right with me playing the field. I don't mean sex but just having a great time with women. They're the best things that have ever been created, but I don't want to settle down with just one of them. There are just too many of them out there to be stuck with just one." He told him he'd better not let Alex or Shipley hear him saying that. "No. You're right on that. I think they'd castrate me or something. But I'm going to happily play the lone bachelor and make sure that no woman feels like I've shafted her by getting married. No sir, marriage and settling down is not for me."

"I hope you change your mind." He told him that he wasn't. That's just the way that he was built, to be a flirt and a lover of women. "I might just tell Shipley what you said just so that we can make fun of you when the right woman comes along for you. Boy, I'm going to tell her too. That'll make for some fun conversations."

As his brothers showed up, their orders were taken for lunch. Dusty wanted to make sure that they met at least once a month like this so that everyone was on the same page when it came to their investments. And he had some great news, too, to go along with the money that they'd made in the last quarter, thanks in part to him being able to think outside the box. And man had he thought outside the box a couple of times this quarter.

Too, if he was right and the other brothers found themselves wives, they'd be a bit more busy and with their own families. He wanted to savor this time with them so that they could still talk about just being brothers. Missing out on any part of their lives would be sad to him. He hoped too that they'd want to get together, too, even after they were old and gray.

After going over all the prior commitments that they had made in the form of investments, he told them about the hospital as well. They had gone ahead and cut the funding that they invested monthly and they were beginning to feel the pinch. He had letters from each of the other board members about how the hospital wasn't working as well as it had before and that their bonuses, huge six-figure ones that he'd not known about, weren't going to be as high this year.

"What I've done is cut the hospital down on their donations again. We're now paying a little less than a quarter of what we were paying them for support over the last several years. If they're getting bonuses because we're donating money, then that has to stop. I feel that they shouldn't be getting any kind of kickback, what I was told that it was, to get new doctors and nurses to come here because we're a state-of-the-art hospital, simply because of our money. Also, The Grable

Foundation will no longer be supporting the wing that was built in Martha's name. I have set it up for maintenance work, but now the bulk of the money, less than half of it, is going to be set up as a fund for nurses and doctors that wish to further their career." Locke asked if he had done this or he was going to. "I did it. There isn't any reason that if we don't agree on this that I couldn't put it back the way it was before. But I will admit that I was angry when I heard the amount of bonus that were going to the board. The very fact that I only just happened upon it, me being a member as well, makes me pissed off. I wonder what the amount was when we were paying everything for those three months when the hospital was in the red."

"I have the amounts." Grinning at his brother, he told him that he had mentioned it to Alex, and they knew that she'd be right on top of things. "I was going to talk to you about it today anyway. I'm sure that we'll all be happy about doing this. The amounts they got was staggering."

After finding out what they were getting in a yearly bonus, he thought about taking more of the funding away. But Knox said that they had to be careful about taking everything away, or they really could make it difficult to have a hospital.

"I've already filed a motion for them to be fined. This is a not-for-profit hospital, and the fact that they're taking profits makes me mad, too. So I've taken legal action against them. Also..." Knox handed out paperwork that he'd collected. "They'll be fired for their parts in the class action suit against them as well. I think that we've been fair with these people and I keep coming back to the fact that we had to tell them that we'd stop funding if they didn't fire a man that they were well aware of him stealing."

"Good. That was going to be my next topic. Also, I've looked into this, and we won't take the money that is awarded to us should we win, other than legal fees. It will all be funneled back into the hospital for funding, such as the nurse and doctor foundation — I don't have a name for it yet so open to that. But I will say that the money awarded will be a godsend to a lot of people and their billings."

After they all agreed that it would be a good way to keep their profits high at home, none of them were keen on the idea of shorting the hospital. It was a place that a great many people used and they were going to need it as well when their baby came along.

Chapter 8

August watched the man trimming around the hedges. It was part of his being here today to go and see the finished project of his design. He didn't want to be here. It was like by coming back, every flaw that he'd made during the construction of the building and landscaping had been right there, front and center to him.

"Mr. Erickson, is there something that I can help you with? Did you find that we've done something wrong with the landscaping?" That was another thing that he hated. Being called Mr. anything, especially Erickson, as that had been what people had called his dad when he'd been alive. And his father no more deserved the respect that came with the title than he felt that he did. He told the man that he was just chilling out. "Well, that's not a good person to chill out to. She's been working here since before the building was put in the ground, I think. Her father and brothers all own the same landscaping company. It was one of the ones that your family recommended to do the work. I think that today, they're just sprucing things up before the big meet and greet tonight. Let me think a moment. It's an odd name. Anyway, Jack, there is the boss to the grounds here, but she'll pick up a tool and work just as hard as her men as well. Mostly men, too. Women, I'd like to say that they're not cut out for this kind of labor and outdoor work but she's right there as a shining example that I'm wrong on that. Or perhaps, what I really think is that she can't fit in with real women and is compensating for it by being a heavy worker like the men. That's what a lot of men think about her, too."

"From here, I thought it was a man." The man might have said something to his statement, but he caught eye of someone storming toward Jack—is that what he called her? And they didn't look all that happy to be around either. "That looks like trouble. Who is that other person? Do you know?"

"That's her mother. The woman striding

toward her, I mean." He nodded, watching as the woman was waving her arms around to no doubt catch the attention of Jack. "They get going at times but I'd hate to be anyone that tried to come between them. Mrs. Blackman — that's it. Blackman Soils. Anyway, they're a close-knit family, but they bicker all the time, too. The old man is set to retire soon. I've heard that he's thinking of leaving it all to his oldest. Now, there is a man that I can get behind. Good guy with a club on the fairways, too."

He didn't comment as the woman, the missus, got closer to the younger Jack. She turned off the weed eater that she was using — he could no longer hear the hum of it from where he was — and stood waiting for the other woman to get to her. It didn't look to him like either of them were giving an inch. While he wouldn't say that they were arguing, it looked to him that the mother was giving her daughter an earful.

August had no idea why he thought that. He couldn't hear their conversation. He wasn't even close enough to tell if they looked alike, either. Didn't know if there were raised voices. Nothing at all about the two of them sent him vibes that he could relate to the two of them. They were just two people that caught his attention on a lawn that he had designed. When the older woman, which he was assuming that as well, turned on her heel and left, Jack stood there watching her. When she turned to look at him, not even a glance but a full minute of looking in his direction, he felt the need to cover his balls. Again, he didn't know why he felt that way. It was just as much there as his love for all things chocolate.

"You'll be staying for the grand opening tonight, won't you? I mean, people will be here from all over the state just to have a good look at what you've done for us here. And it's a damned good job too. Everything about this place, from the building to the lawns, is top shelf." He told the man that he and two of his brothers were coming. "Good. Hey, if you wanted to know anything about Jack, she's single. Pretty too. If you go for that kind of pretty. But she's hard on a man. I've never tried, but I'm assuming from others that she doesn't date many men. Perhaps that's the trouble with her. She doesn't particularly care for men. I can't think of another reason why she'd be turned off by the boss like I am."

"What do you mean?" When he didn't get an answer, he had to drag his focus from Jack to the man beside him to get an answer. "Why would you say that? I think that all women are beautiful."

"Jack is one of those natural women. You know what I mean, I'm sure. A wealthy man like you gets around, I'm betting." Again, he had to ask him what he meant. "You know. No makeup. Hair hanging down past her ass. She's in good shape, I'll give her that but I'm not into that sort of female. I'd like for mine to put up a fuss about what she's wearing and has make up on. You know? Stylish women that I can sink my teeth into when I need a blowjob or something. Not that kind of woman that would take over sex like it's their thing."

"No, actually, I haven't any idea what you're talking about. And I don't think that it's very smart of you to be talking about someone who is in your employment. Especially with that tone." He put up his hands and backed away, telling him that he was only making an observation. "Perhaps this Jack person would like to know what you think about her ass and lack of makeup. I have a feeling that she'd either slap you or tell you to fuck off."

"I was only making conversation, Mr.

Erickson. I'm sorry if I offended you. I guess you go for that kind of woman, then. One that tells you what they like and how you're to move. Bossy bitches." He told him that he hadn't offended him but women in general. "Christ, who shit in your cereal? I was just making conversation and to find out if you're coming to this thing tonight. If you ask me, I'd rather you stay at home than be a stick in the mud about a woman who is too dense to get herself a real job and to dress up once in a while before she becomes as old as my grandmama and still not plucked." He turned and punched the man in the face before he could say another word.

August had no idea why he'd hit the man. Well, he had an idea, but it was still messing with his mind that he'd care enough about a woman that he didn't even know to come to her aide. If his sisters-in-law were here, they'd take him to task after they'd hit the man, too. He needed to get out of here before he decided to defend the janitorial service. There had been a few women in that department as well. There was something wrong with him, he decided. Something so wrong with him that he was beating up men that were not worth the effort of getting his hands dirty for.

Getting in his car to head back to his hotel room, he drove slowly by Jack as she was talking to a group of men. He waved at them when they turned to look in his direction. He told himself several times that he wasn't just waving at the woman but at the group of them as they stood there. He wondered what his family would say to him if they found out that he had a passing interest in a stranger. They'd have his head on a pike if he said one word about her.

After tearing his tie off, August decided that he needed to do something physical. He was going to change into something loose fitting—he was going to be dressed up enough tonight as the affair was black tie tonight. He decided that he'd hit up the gym and have some downtime.

Demitrius and Zander were going to be joining him tonight, and he hoped the fuck that they kept their mouths shut about— Thinking about where his mind had been going, August stopped on the treadmill, nearly killing himself when it kept moving.

He'd been thinking about defending her against his brothers. Not so much defending her but keeping them away from her so that...so that he could what, he asked himself. He couldn't even pick her out of a crowd, much less talk to her when they were at the dinner tonight. Then he had to wonder if she'd be there.

By the time his brothers showed up, he had decided not to go for about the hundredth time. He had too much on his mind to get himself into a situation not of his doing. August just knew that he was going to be in trouble for hitting the man from earlier and didn't want to have to deal with the consequences of that or the man. Of course, that didn't sit well with either of his brothers. They'd been looking forward to this thing all month, so they were able to bully him into going anyway.

"I want to say right now that I'm not going to be looking at any women." Zander laughed at him and asked him since when was he going to be doing that. "I'm just putting it out there that I'm in no mood to find myself a woman tonight, and I want to get an early start back home in the morning, so I want you two to behave as well."

Looking at himself in the mirrored wall in the elevator, he thought that he pulled off his disinterested face quite well. The three of them together, all of them in black ties and tails, took on an air of going to the prom, he thought. Not that he'd ever been to a prom, none of them had but he did feel like he was embarking on something that was going to have him in trouble. How? He didn't know, but again, he was baffled by where his train of thought was going and decided that he wasn't going to drink either. That's all he needed was to add alcohol to his already fucked up head.

He saw the man that he'd hit earlier as he stood at the bar and flirted. He was going on about how he'd gotten the black eye and busted lip in the gym. He said that he was playing pickle with some buddies. All he did was walk up to the bar and had the man, he couldn't remember his name, walk away. The bartender thanked him.

"He's been pestering me since I was setting up here. I thought that there was some kind of rule about staff and employers, but apparently, he didn't get the memo." He told her that he'd hang out with her so that he got the message. "Thanks, but I have my pepper spray. He'll either get it or not. I hope he doesn't, in a way."

Asking for a glass of water, determined that he was going to stay sober, he nearly swallowed his tongue when a woman walked into the room.

He couldn't think of a single thing to compare her to other than the sun setting or even the most beautiful rose. She was dressed for sex, and that was all he could think about.

The woman was dressed head to toe in red. It even sparkled when she moved, and she was so lovely in it. There was nothing left for him to imagine, either. As he'd thought before, she was sex in a tight-fitting red dress, and he wanted to make sure that she wasn't wearing anything beneath the dress as he could imagine him touching her.

He looked at the bartender when she said his name. Looking at her, his mind fuzzy again. She had to repeat herself twice before he understood what she was telling him. Christ, he thought, he was a dead man.

"Her name is Jacklynn Blackham. She goes by Jack. To see her working, you'd never know that she was one of the workers on this project just today." He asked her how she knew her. "She's my Aunt, my mom's much younger sister. She told me about this job so I could make some money for college. She didn't tell me that every man here would be hitting on me, but I guess that's par for the course."

Jack moved to the bar where he was and started talking to the younger woman behind the setup. If they were speaking English, he didn't understand a word they were saying. All he could think about was the small part of a tattoo that he saw coming out of the back of her dress as it made its way lazily down her arm to just under her breast.

"Do I have something in my teeth?" He moved his eyes along her body to her mouth and moaned. She grabbed his chin and pulled it up so that he was looking into her furious eyes. "What is the matter with you? Are you stupid?"

"No. I'm not..." He looked at the woman behind the bar again, then at Jack. "I'm not sure what is wrong with me. To be honest with you, all I can think about is where that tattoo leads and if there is any way that I can convince you to allow me to see it."

She stared at him for several minutes. He didn't dare glance around, fearful that if he did, she'd knock him on his ass. When she asked him if he was August Erickson, he couldn't speak but he did nod.

"Did anyone ever teach you manners where

you're from?" He said that he didn't know what was wrong with him and that he had indeed been taught that what he was thinking and feeling wasn't right. "I don't even want to know what you're talking about. I'm just here because my mother told me that if I didn't come that I'd be blacklisted for other jobs. Now I have the main man of the night ogling me like I'm some sort of plaything that he'd like to get in a dark corner."

"Don't." She asked him what he said. "Don't talk about dark corners. My mind is centered enough on figuring out where I can take you to kiss you out of that dress. Christ, and I heard that you were pretty. You're everything but pretty. You're the most gorgeous woman that I've ever laid eyes on. And that dress? I had no idea that black tie meant that I'd be barely able to control myself. I might well have gone to these a good deal sooner. No, that wouldn't have worked. You wouldn't have been there when I was."

"Are you hitting on me?" He smiled and laughed a little, telling her that he was indeed. "Why? I mean, you've gone on about my dress. You can have it if you want to. I don't particularly care for it or the color. It's very red."

"It is at that. And let me be as honest with you as you are to me. I'd rather see you out of the dress than anything that I've ever done." She stared at him and then threw back her head and laughed. He wasn't sure but he thought that bells were the only thing to come to mind when she laughed again. "You're very beautiful. I hope you are aware of that. Every man in here is drooling over you. Women, too, I would imagine."

They talked the entire night. He saw the man that he'd hit, Bill Ward she told him try to avoid him. But feeling the way that he was, he headed toward the man with Jack on his arm. He asked him if his face hurt.

"Not at all." He touched his finger to his nose and winced a bit. "I hurt it today. I was just about to come and see who this lovely creature is that is looking about as bored as I was this afternoon when we were talking."

"It's Jack." He took a sip of his water while watching Bill. "You remember her from this afternoon. You were telling me what you think about her ass and lack of makeup. You might not have said the words, but I had a feeling that you found her to be lacking."

"You said that about me?" Bill nodded, then shook his head. "I'm assuming from your tone that you defended my honor. Thank you for that. But in the future, I fight my own battles."

He didn't see her move. One second, she was glaring at Bill. The next, Bill was on the floor with his arm up under him in an odd way. Taking Jack's hand, he pulled her away from the scene before anyone else noticed and found them a dark room. Christ, if he wasn't turned on by her before, he certainly was now.

As soon as the door was closed behind them, he pressed her against the door and took her mouth. She was pulling at his tie when he finally found the little snap that held the dress together around her neck. Her breasts, he'd been right; she had nothing on beneath it, spilled into his hands, and he pulled them both up to his mouth.

"Hurry." He didn't know if he could move any faster, but when she dropped to her knees in front of him, her lovely body only highlighted by the small light in the plug, he nearly killed himself trying to help her pull his pants off. August nearly fell backward when she took his cock into her mouth and swallowed him past the tightness of her throat.

~*~

All she could think about was touching this man. She wanted him to fuck her hard, take her gently, and to eat her as she needed to be taken. Christ, she'd never been so hot for someone as she was this nearly complete stranger. Cupping his balls into her hand, giving them a gentle but firm grasp, she was startled out of her need when he pulled her up from the floor.

"I need to be inside of you." She nodded and found herself turned with her back to him and leaning over what she thought was a laundry bin. It didn't matter. Even if it had been the wash tub that she could see, too, she'd let him take her. As he entered her, Jack came. Over and over until she was dizzy with it. "Come again. I need to feel you wrapped around me when I come."

She slid her fingers into her pussy, making it tighter than it had already been for him. As soon as she slid her finger over his cock head, he leaned over her and took her breasts into his hands. Even as he was coming, both of them making enough noise to wake the dead, she found that she didn't care so long as this man was giving her all that she needed.

He fucked her through two more mind-blowing releases. Her body, her breasts especially, were tender and well-loved. As he turned her around, pulling out of her pussy long enough to enter her again, she leaned heavily on him as he lifted her up from the floor.

This time their fucking, no other word for what they were doing. He was softer, easier on her body. She came so many times, each one of them taking her breath away while he fucked her. She was going to be sore tomorrow and found that she didn't care at all.

"I wondered what your tat looked like." She grinned at him, telling him that few people got to see the whole thing. "Good. I like that. While I have no doubt that you can tell me to fuck off, I'd like to see you again. And again. And again."

While he traced her tat with his fingers, she began to realize what they'd done. They'd had... well fuck. She just had unprotected sex with a man she'd only just met.

"Christ." She looked up at him. They were about the same height, but she liked that she didn't have to look down on him. "I just realized that I came here with my brothers. They're going to... not that I will ever tell them, but they will wonder what I've been up to."

She felt embarrassed. Looking for her dress, she felt her eyes fill with tears. Before she could turn her back on him, August pressed her against the door again after pulling on his pants. He lifted her chin up so that he was looking into her eyes.

"Don't cry, baby." She burst into tears and only just realized that she was hurt for the dumbest reasons. Telling him that she didn't want him to be embarrassed about her, she clung to him while she cried. "On honey, I'd shout it from the roof if that would make you feel better. I just meant that I'd hate for them to find us here when they'd come looking. I don't want anyone else to see this loveliness that is you."

She laughed. "Good save. I'm sorry." He asked her for what. "I don't know, really. But I want you to know that I've never in my life done anything like this before. I'm not easy." He kissed her.

"This is my first time as well. At least in a utility cabinet. I hope it won't be the last either." She laughed again. "There you go. I love your laughter. I was thinking that it reminded me of bells ringing."

"Don't be a sap." He stiffened slightly, and she asked him what was wrong. His smile was anything but reassuring to her. "What? You just had sex — the most incredible sex in the world with me. The least you can do is be honest with me."

"I have a lot of brothers. Five of them. And just before I left, my older brother was saying how he wished that I'd fall in love with someone so that I'd know how he felt with his new wife." She asked him if he was proposing to her now. "I don't know. Would you marry me?"

"No." She was hurt when he nodded. "You aren't serious, are you? I mean, we just met. I know that is stupid to say since we're both nearly naked and had some great sex — I can't tell you enough how great that was, but we just met." He turned her around and helped to snap her dress back in place. It was still good-looking, but her hair was a mess.

When she turned back around, she looked at the man. Good heavens, he was a handsome thing. Putting her finger close to his cheek, wanting to leave her lipstick there and not, he took her hand into his and kissed it. She didn't know what to think when he did that.

"I'm confused as to what I want. I do want to marry you. I don't know why I think that's a good thing, but that's how I feel." She told him then that she wasn't on any kind of birth control either. "Good. Again, I don't know why, but I'd…you'd tell me if we made our child tonight, wouldn't you?"

"Yes." She couldn't think beyond this man being so nice to her when all she wanted to do was to go home and sob. "I don't know if I want to smack you or love you. I can't think right now."

"That's good. At least we're on the same page." She laughed when he did. "I'll go out first. I'm sure that someone is going to miss us soon. But I'll make sure that the coast is clear and you can go to the bathroom to fix, while still lovely, fix your hair and makeup so that you don't have to be embarrassed."

True to his word, he knocked on the door when she could come out. Racing to the bathroom with her heels in her hand, she went into the bathroom and locked the door behind her. Standing in the stall, Jack sobbed for everything that had happened to her. Putting her hand on her flat tummy, she thought of the possibility that a child could be there.

"Just so you know. If he abandons us, we'll be just fine. You and I are going to be a team, and no one is going to call you a one-night-stand baby." She knew that she was talking out of her head and finally got up the courage to go to the mirror. "Not so bad."

After scrubbing off her makeup, she stared at herself in the mirror. She looked abused but in a good way. Her lips were swollen, there was a small hickey on her throat that she smiled about, and she'd at some point lost her panties. Not that they were all that much anyway.

Giving herself a good talking to, knowing that August had left the building by now, she opened the door and nearly fell back when the man of the hour was standing there. He pushed her back into the bathroom and kissed her gently on the mouth.

"I thought that you'd be gone." He told her that he didn't want to leave without her. "But your brothers. Won't they be pissed off with you when you tell them...I have no idea what you'd tell them."

"I told them that I'd gotten hung up and that they were to leave without me. I think that they were ready to go anyway. I've ordered us a car. I don't know where you live but we're to meet the car around the back. That way, no one will see us leaving." She asked him if he was going to go back to the party. "No. As I said, I don't want to be anywhere without you."

The limo, a sleek black long one, was pulling up as the two of them exited the building. She could have kissed the driver when he tipped his hat at her, asking her if she was ready to leave. He didn't say a word about how either of them were dressed. August had given her his coat to put over her dress as it had started to rain.

"I don't know about you, but I'm starving. I hope you don't mind, but I've asked the driver to take us through a drive-thru. I don't know what it is you feel like, but I could eat about a dozen burgers right now." She was happy to have something to eat as well and nearly didn't taste the first burger that she ate.

"I thought you'd be a steak man." She asked him what his favorite food was when he was out.

He told her that he had a brother that was a chef so they were all subject to all kinds of foods. "Do you like salads?"

"Salads? I can eat them. I don't know that I'd go out of my way to have one. But yeah, I can eat them." She told him how her mother was forever on her about not eating better. "That's me too. My sister-in-law, Alex, she's big on us all eating better. I grab what I can when I can. I seem to be on the move a great deal."

"I burn a great deal of energy when I'm working. I'm a hands-on kind of boss. My dad is the same way. But he's retiring soon, and when he does, he'll leave the business to one of my brothers. I'm the youngest by a lot." She told him things about her family that she'd not thought of before. "Richard is about as useless as my mom is when it comes to cooking in the kitchen. So, since he's the oldest, he'll more than likely take over the business. If that happens, I'm going to leave for greener pastures, so to speak. I don't mind him getting it but I don't think that I could work with him and still like him. David is the same way. Not very hands-on."

"We grew up poor, the six of us. My brother,

he played the lottery about once a week and we won a good deal of money." They talked for what seemed like hours. Even after getting back to her hotel room, not wanting to drive back to her home, she changed into her comfy clothing and sat in the living room suite and talked to him.

She'd never had so much fun as she was tonight. Jack only hoped that she'd been right in saying that it wasn't going to be a one-night stand. Not with this man.

Before You Go...

HELP AN AUTHOR
write a review
THANK YOU!

Share your voice and help guide other readers to these wonderful books. Even if it's only a line or two, your reviews help readers discover the author's books so they can continue creating stories that you'll love. Log in to your favorite retailer and leave a review. Thank you.

AWARD WINNING, BESTSELLING AUTHOR

Kathi Barton, a winner of the Pinnacle Book Achievement Award and a best-selling author on Amazon and All Romance books, lives in Nashport, Ohio, with her husband, Paul. When not creating new worlds and romance, Kathi and her husband enjoy camping and going to auctions. She can also be seen at county fairs with her husband, an artist and potter.

Her muse, a cross between Jimmy Stewart and Hugh Jackman, brings her stories to life for her readers in a way that has them coming back time and again for more. Her favorite genre is paranormal romance, with a great deal of spice. You can visit Kathi online and drop her an email if you'd like. She loves hearing from her fans. aaronskiss@gmail.com.

Follow Kathi on her blog: http://kathisbartonauthor.blogspot.com/